Also By Shan

The Pet Psychic Series

Karma's a Bitch

Lady Luck Runs Out

Silence Is Golden

For Pete's Sake

Pushing Up Daisies

Paws & Pose Mysteries

Faux Pas

High Jinx

Dog Gone

Frankie O'Farrell Mysteries

Buried in the Dark

Missing in the Dark

The Burning

Her Little Secret

A Novel

Shannon Esposito

misterio press

Copyright © Shannon Esposito, 2023

Published by misterio press

Printed in The United States of America

This book is a work of fiction. Names, characters, places and incidents either are products of the author's imagination or are used fictitiously. Any resemblance to actual events or locales or persons, living or dead, is entirely coincidental.

All rights reserved. Except as permitted under the U.S. Copyright Act of 1976, no part of this publication may be reproduced, distributed or transmitted in any form or by any means, or stored in a database or retrieval system, without the prior written permission of the publisher.

* * * * *

Visit Shannon Esposito's official website at: http://murderinparadise.com

* * * * *

Cover Art by Dar Albert

Formatting by Debora Lewis/deboraklewis@yahoo.com

* * * * *

ISBN: 978-1-947287-55-6

For Dan, for your unwavering faith in me.

Prologue

20 Years Ago

Mila stirred in the darkness as her eyes fluttered and popped open. Her heart leaped around like a caged sparrow in her chest, her nervous system on high alert, and she didn't know why. As she worked on slowing her breathing, she clutched the patchwork quilt—a gift from her Grandma Mary when she'd left for college—and yanked it up to her chin. Light from a full moon seeped between the blinds, and as her eyes adjusted, shadows in the small bedroom began to take shape. Oak dresser with mirror, nightstand, laundry basket. Nothing out of place.

Did she have a bad dream?

A dog's lonely howl echoed in the distance. A car raced through the neighborhood, exhaust backfiring, making her jump. The bedroom window was cracked open to let in the cool night air. Maybe that wasn't such a good idea, but Florida winter nights brought cooler temps, so Mila and her college roommate, Sabine, took advantage of that to turn off the AC and save on the electric bill.

Had a noise outside jarred her awake? Maybe Sabine had gotten up to use the bathroom or grabbed a late-night snack from the kitchen. Yeah, that had to be it.

Her heart rate finally began to slow. With a sigh, she tried to relax back into sleep.

Mila's dad had discovered this two-bedroom Hyde Park bungalow for rent after she'd found out she'd been accepted to the University of Tampa, and Sabine had answered the ad for a roommate the same day Mila had posted it. They'd clicked instantly, becoming inseparable in the past year, both getting jobs at The Meat Market on the weekend, a fancy steakhouse where people tipped well. Mila felt close to someone again for the first time since losing her older sister three years ago.

Tonight they'd joined a group of friends after work at The Retreat for a few games of pool and darts. Tomorrow the plan was to go to the Farmer's Market, get some local veggies for soup and then hunker down and study. They both had big exams coming up before the holiday break. Mila's least favorite subject was statistics and her grades reflected that. She had to ace this exam.

With a groan, Mila reached over and checked the time on her phone. 3:14 a.m. She'd only slept for an hour. Just as she felt her eyes get heavy again, a muffled thump made her sit up. Quilt held protectively up to her chin, she stared at her closed door, straining to hear beyond it.

Was that a male voice?

Sabine's boyfriend, Lucas, had a key and she had mentioned he might come over. It was probably him.

Another thump, like something heavy had fallen on the wood floor. *Was that a muffled cry?* Mila held her breath, listening harder. A few quieter thuds. Those were not normal nightly sounds. *What was going on?*

Insides trembling, Mila grabbed her phone, punched in 911 just in case she needed to hit enter and then slipped out of bed. She opened the bedroom door as quietly as she could and peered into the living room. Nothing seemed out of place. The front door was closed. She tiptoed across the room, feeling exposed and vulnerable, and quickly checked the door. Locked.

Arms crossed, phone clutched like a lifeline in her hand, she maneuvered around the flowered Goodwill couch and slowly made her way toward Sabine's bedroom. The tiny kitchen was to her right and she glanced in as she passed. The stained-glass, palm tree night light next to the sink was lit as usual. No sign of the noises coming from anything that had fallen in there. No sign Sabine had made a late-night snack. She wasn't the neatest person, so there was usually evidence. Their shared bathroom was to her left. She looked in. The shower curtain was pulled back and nothing was out of place in there either.

At the end of the hall, Sabine's door stood cracked open, moonlight casting a rectangle of light on the dark hardwood floor. There was a shuffling noise coming from behind the door. She paused. *Maybe Lucas had come in, and she was about to interrupt them?* Well, she had to check now that she was up and freaked out. A little embarrassment was worth a good night's sleep.

Moving forward, she slowly pushed open the door. "Sabine?"

The scene that greeted her was something from her nightmares. The window stood wide open, blowing the gauzy white curtain and letting in enough moonlight for Mila to take it all in. A scream stuck in her throat as her brain tried to comprehend what she was seeing.

Sabine lay face down on the bed, nude except for her white tank-top, which was stained with blood, along with her sheets. The one visible, glistening blue eye was staring, unseeing, past Mila.

A man with a black ski mask stood in the room, an intruder with one hand in her dresser drawer, and a large kitchen butcher knife clutched in the other hand. Time seemed to stand still as they stood frozen, staring at each other.

Mila couldn't get her legs to move. She couldn't pull her eyes away from the blood on that knife, and she couldn't push the scream past her constricted throat.

And then he lunged toward her. In two wide steps, he was in front of her. He was tall, around the same height as her father, sloped shoulders, thin build. She could smell the coppery, earthy scent of blood, could see the pleasure gleaming in his black eyes as he grabbed her arm, fingers digging into her flesh, and swung the knife toward her face.

She turned and felt a burn as it caught her above her jawbone, next to her ear and sliced down her neck. Her adrenalin kicked in and she finally released the scream that had been lodged in her throat. At the same time, her phone clattered to the floor.

As he pulled back his arm, holding the knife up and bringing it down toward her chest again like an icepick, her muscle memory kicked in. She'd spent the last ten years making Krav Maga part of her daily workouts.

Her right arm shot out, bent at an angle, palm out, blocking his forearm and keeping distance between her and the bloody knife. At the same time, she poked him in the eye with the fingers in her left hand and when he stumbled back, she landed a hard kick between his legs. She felt the jolt of physical contact from her foot up into her spine. Her brain was on high alert, registering every second, every sensation.

"You bitch," he wheezed, bent over.

Mila took the opportunity to kick him again, this time aiming at the hand holding the knife. *Contact.* It flew from his hand and slid beneath the dresser.

Just then they heard the front door open.

Mila held her stance, her chest heaving, her vision like a tunnel locked on the man half bent over, breathing as hard as she was, his gaze darting behind her. As footsteps came toward them, he glanced at her once more, hate burning in his eyes and then turned and scrambled out of the open window.

With a sob, Mila stumbled over to Sabine. She brushed the blonde hair stained with blood off her face and pressed her fingers into her friend's neck to check for a pulse. No surprise there wasn't one. But she had hoped.

"Oh my God!" Lucas was suddenly there, on his knees beside her, his large hand cradling Sabine's face. "Oh my God! Sabine!" His cries and sobs echoed off the bedroom walls as Mila forced her jelly legs to carry her the few feet to where her phone had landed against the wall. Her voice sounded far away and foreign to her as she told the 911 operator her best friend was dead.

She felt nothing as the blood ran down her neck, soaking her T-shirt.

One

Rojo spotted his prey. A cluster of sanderlings skittered around on tiny legs, poked their black bills into the wet sand. The flock of white-bellied shore birds moved in unison with the rhythm of the incoming waves, taunting and teasing the dog's prey drive.

The sixty-pound boxer mix strained against the leash, gagging himself.

Crystal struggled to hold him. "Okay, okay. Hang on." Her dog's muscles quivered as she unclipped his leash. Once freed, he took off in great strides, sand flying behind his hind paws, gleefully sending the tiny birds into flight.

"Stupid mutt," Benny chuckled beside her. "Too dumb to know he ain't never gonna catch one."

Crystal narrowed her eyes. Eyes that felt like sandpaper from crying. Harsh morning light glinted off the ocean, causing silver spots like confetti in her vision.

Maybe that's the secret to happiness. Not knowing you'll never get what you want. Ignorance.

She reached up and slipped a gold heart pendant from beneath her T-shirt collar, rubbing it back and forth between her thumb and forefinger. This had been her ritual for ten years now when, like today, she needed courage or comfort. It had been a gift from her dad for her twenty-first birthday, along with advice about never giving her heart to a man unworthy of it.

It definitely wasn't the man she'd given it to.

She tried to ignore the nausea churning her gut and concentrated instead on the cool, packed sand beneath her bare feet. The ocean was calm for now, two-foot waves rolling in one at a time, morphing from the color of green sea glass to whitewash as they broke on the shore. The impermanence and destruction weren't lost on her. That seemed to be the theme of her life.

Normally she took this early morning beach walk with Rojo, but today she'd asked Benny, her boyfriend of five years, to join them. Last night had been the last straw. She'd cooked a spaghetti dinner with meatballs, his favorite, and even bought some cute candles at the Dollar Store, thinking they could have a romantic dinner for once. But he'd gone to Whiskey Joe's with his Pro Star Construction coworkers instead. Didn't even bother to call and let her know. Just didn't come home until the spaghetti was congealed and the candles burned down.

A shudder ran through her as she recalled being woken from a dead sleep by his whiskey-soaked tongue pushing into her mouth. She'd managed to squirm away and lock herself in the bathroom until he'd passed out, snoring and drooling on her pillow. Then she'd told herself, as she'd wrapped her arms around Rojo on the sofa, tears darkening his fur, that she deserved better and would kick Benny's sorry, drunken butt to the curb in the morning.

But, in the light of day, as they made their way down the beach in strained silence, she couldn't shake the image of the pickle jar that had come flying at her the last time she'd asked him to move out. That was ten stitches to her forehead and an embarrassing morning of nurses and doctors side-eyeing her when she'd insisted she'd fallen.

She lifted her chin, letting the salty breeze push the overdue-for-a-cut fringe from her eyes, then she pulled her shoulders back, trying to feel confident.

Fake it 'til you make it, Crystal. You got this.

Seagulls squawked in warning as Rojo stalked them; rising in a cloud of feathers and angry screeches when he barked and lunged. He glanced back at her, tongue hanging from an open mouth. He sure looked like he was smiling. *Oh, to be a dog.*

Benny cleared his throat like he wanted to say something. Crystal glanced at him. She couldn't see his eyes behind the dark Ray-Bans, but she could see the tight line of his mouth and the tension in his shoulders. He knew this wasn't just a casual morning walk together.

As she avoided stepping in a mound of fishy-smelling, brown seaweed, she suddenly became aware of the emptiness of the long stretch of beach. Normally, the quiet would soothe her. Today it felt like a threat.

The morning sky was a flat blue, crisp like a fresh start. She really needed a fresh start. Next month, the snowbirds would return to Edgewater and there would be some swimsuit-clad vacationers dotting the beach at this hour, fishing, searching for shells and sharks' teeth. But in September, it was still hers and Rojo's. That's the reason she liked to bring Rojo here in the morning, so he could run off-leash without anyone complaining, but maybe an isolated stretch of beach wasn't the best spot to try to break up with Benny.

"Look," Benny said, his gruff voice in the silence startling her. "I know I need to cut back on the drinkin', okay? You don't have to say nothin'. You know I just need to blow off some steam, right?"

Crystal's insides began to tremble. She rubbed the heart pendant more aggressively. *How could he be so clueless? Cut back on the drinking?* His solution was so far from what she needed, she was stunned into silence.

Rojo loped back to them, nudged her hand with his blocky head like he knew she needed support. He licked her arm, then circled them and took off again after a group of gulls. Since her dad was gone, Rojo was the only male she could count on.

"You're not going to get all dramatic about this, are you?" Benny huffed, his sunglasses facing her, dark greasy hair sticking up from his wide forehead. "People drink, Crys. That's how they deal with stress. It's normal. But I'll cut back for you. Cause you don't like it."

Crystal felt the blood rising to her face, her stomach burning with acid. "Don't do me any favors." The breeze swept away her meager words, her mousy voice, like smoke.

"What's that?" he barked. "You gettin' smart with me? Cause I don't need to take your shit, Crys. I got plenty of women would be glad to be in your place."

Crystal watched her toes with peeling red polish leave an impression in the sand with each step, bit her tongue. This was escalating and she hadn't even got to break up with him yet. No, she couldn't do it here. She'd have to get him in a more public place and do it there. With witnesses.

Suddenly Rojo let out a string of urgent, sharp yips. Both their heads swiveled in his direction. He was sitting in front of the old, rickety lifeguard stand by the edge of the dunes, head tilted back, whining. Then he circled the small structure, nose to the ground. It hadn't been used for a decade, except for the occasion teen couple making out or sharing a six-pack of beer.

"Wonder if an animal crawled up there and died?" Benny changed direction and trudged through the deeper sand toward the old stand.

Crystal glanced up at two vultures lazily gliding in a circling pattern above them and then followed behind Benny unenthusiastically. A dead animal was the last thing she wanted to see, especially as depressed as she already felt.

As they approached the weathered, wooden structure with peeling blue paint, Benny lifted himself onto his toes, trying to see into the shadows beyond the opening. It was too high off the ground. There were two windows to the left of the door, facing the ocean, but a layer of salt and grime made them opaque.

Crystal crossed her arms, an uneasiness tightening her chest. Rojo was now on his belly, scooting under the structure to sniff the sand. It was a puddle of darkness. "Rojo, get out of there. Come here, boy."

Shining brown eyes glanced back at her, but whatever he smelled was too enticing to resist.

There was a rotted set of wooden stairs in the front, the first three steps missing. Benny was stretching his foot toward the fourth step, his hands gripping the eroded railings.

"Benny, are you sure that's a good idea?" Crystal hugged herself harder. She had a really bad feeling about this. She didn't want to live with the man anymore, but she didn't want him to fall and bust his head open either.

As Benny made his way carefully up the six or so remaining steps, she urgently called for Rojo, trying to sound stern but only managing to sound panicked. The dog was snuffling in the dark shadows and completely ignoring her.

Suddenly Benny shouted and came tumbling back down the stairs, landing on his back with a thud in the sand.

"Oh, God!" Both Crystal and Rojo raced over and stared down at him. Crystal snapped the leash on Rojo while she had the chance, eyeing a dark brown stain on his muzzle. "What happened? What's wrong?"

Benny's sunglasses had fallen off, his bloodshot eyes were wide with fear. "Call 911. It's a girl. A ... dead girl."

Crystal felt the blood drain from her head as she glanced up at the now menacing lifeguard stand. She wanted to run, but there were prickling stars in her vision and the sky began to spin. Her legs gave out. She plopped down in the sand, her head between her knees. Somewhere in the distance, Benny was yelling at her to call 911.

Two

An oscillating fan pulled the morning breeze from the Gulf waters into the garage as Detective Mila Harlow wiped the sweat from her eyes with her forearm, and then returned to the punching bag. *Boom boom.* Her therapy was the *thwap* of her left and then her right fist striking the bag as she practiced a double-up hook to the head. She moved to a shoulder roll and upper hook. *Thwap. Boom boom,* hook, hook, shoulder roll, upper hook. A mantra that cleared her mind, swept away the ghosts that haunted her while she became only her striking fists, her twisting torso, her powerful legs.

Four years ago this house, a baby blue Victorian built in the 1900's, had been willed to Mila by her Grandma Mary upon her death. Her grandparents on her mother's side, Mary and Gene, had lived in this house since their marriage in 1941. This garage had once held Mila and her siblings' bikes, skimboards, fishing poles and other toys of their childhood so when they'd spend summers here in Edgewater, they were never bored. It had been like summer camp without a schedule. Freedom. That's what she'd always felt as she and her three siblings waved goodbye to their parents from the driveway. Now, this garage held the tools to keep her strong enough to do her job safely. It was a different form of freedom.

Suddenly she noticed the air had changed behind her, the sound of the fan had dampened. She pivoted on her right heel, her left leg shooting out in a controlled, lightning-fast sidekick, freezing with her foot locked in the air.

"You're getting slow," Paul said as he placed a hand on her sneaker, which had stopped inches from his face, and lowered it. "We've been standing here for at least twenty seconds." He glanced down at his K-9 partner, a three-year-old Malinois with an intense stare panting beside him. "Isn't that right, Max?"

Max gave a soft woof.

Mila dropped her leg and pulled off her fingerless, leather boxing gloves, ignoring how good Paul looked in a tight black T-shirt and blue jeans. His stress relief was pumping iron at the gym, and it showed. It'd been five years since the divorce, and they'd settled into a nice rhythm with their daughter. She didn't want to ruin that just because he could still get her heart pumping. But he was right. She'd been lost in thought and let her guard down.

"Good to see *you* at least, Max." She scratched the dog under his long muzzle, getting a string of saliva on her arm for the effort. Then she frowned at her ex-husband. "You're early." She grabbed a towel, wiped the sweat from her face then the saliva from her arm. "Harper and Kittie are probably still working on breakfast."

"Well, then I'd say we're just in time." He rarely smiled, but when he did, it was genuine, lighting up his whole face. She couldn't help but smile back.

She shook her head as she followed him inside.

They'd met at Bradenton Police Academy after college, and the first time she'd looked into his blue eyes she was reminded of the ocean: the only place that felt safe, that felt like home. They had loved each other deeply and recklessly. If she was being honest, they still did. But their jobs were all-consuming, leaving nothing left at the end of the day to give to a marriage. Especially two years in when they were both still working patrol, and Mila had gotten pregnant, despite being on the pill. She'd never wanted children. Not because she didn't like them, but because it terrified her to be responsible for protecting something she would love that much. Especially a daughter. The anxiety of bringing a daughter into a world where one in four girls was sexually assaulted made her spiral. They fought about everything concerning Harper. Mila's fear made her lash out at the one person closest to her... Paul.

When Harper was three, Paul had moved to Clearwater PD, an hour and a half away from them. She couldn't blame him. He had no idea how to handle Mila's anxiety and besides, it was a chance for him to eventually move into the K-9 Unit, his dream job. Their marriage survived two more years apart, probably because they *were* apart, before calling it quits. She tried not to blame herself. After all, when cops marry cops it's nearly a hundred percent divorce rate. Against all odds is not just a challenge, it's a promise.

Paul's mother, Kittie, had retired from teaching at that time and offered to help with Harper, so Mila had time to train to be a detective, *her* dream job. And then after Grandma Mary passed and left her this house in Edgewater, she'd decided to move Harper here. A smaller, safer town, a slower way of life. Kittie had moved with them. Kittie and Mila had always been close and besides, Kittie's only grandchild was her whole world.

Mila had applied for an open patrol position in Edgewater first. It was a quieter job than the four years she'd spent as a General Crimes Detective at Sarasota PD. Things finally felt like they were falling into place. The less demanding job, along with Kittie's support, allowed Mila space to finally start to work on her trauma and anxiety in therapy. Not that she wasn't still over-protective and over-vigilant with Harper, but at least the panic attacks had become rare. When one of the Edgewater detectives retired two years ago, Captain Bartol had offered her the position. It hadn't hurt that Captain Bartol and Grandma Mary had been in the same bridge club. Small towns had strong loyalties.

Mila took a quick cold shower, blow-dried her shoulder-length, dark bob and threw on a fresh pair of black running shorts and cotton "Life is Good" T-shirt. As she refastened the dainty, silver quarter moon necklace around her neck, she met her own gaze in the mirror—opaque green eyes with gold flecks, dark lashes, haunted and uninviting. "Be the light," she whispered.

In the aftermath of Sabine's murder, Mila had dropped out of college and stayed with her grandma. One particularly hard night a few months into a spell of clinical depression, Grandma Mary had walked her out to the backyard to look at the night sky and full moon. They'd stood there in the swampy summer air, swatting at mosquitoes for a full five minutes before Grandma Mary's voice broke the silence. "The world is full of darkness, yes," she'd said. "But you don't have to be a part of that. You, my dearest, are the moon, the light that helps others navigate that darkness."

The next day Mila had decided—to her father's dismay—to switch from psychology to a criminal justice degree before heading off to the police academy. Following in her father's footsteps, something she never thought she would do, strained their relationship to the breaking point. He still didn't understand or support her decision, though he believed she did get something good out of it... Paul. And then she screwed that up, too.

Paul, Kittie and Harper were still sitting at the table when she entered the kitchen, remnants of Sunday morning pancakes, eggs and bacon littering their plates, the sweet scent of maple syrup hanging in the air.

Harper, her ten-year-old daughter, watched her with a sly smile. "We saved you some blueberry pancakes. Dad was just telling us about the time Max jumped through broken glass in a truck window to get a bad guy who ran from Dad and had meth. Pulled him right out through the window."

"Really?" Mila shot Paul a look as she lowered herself into the chair between Harper and Kittie, pressing a kiss into her daughter's crown, getting a whiff of her strawberry-scented shampoo. "I'm not sure that's an appropriate story. A ten-year-old shouldn't have *meth* in their vocabulary."

Kittie passed her the plate of blueberry pancakes with a wink. "Mila's right, Paul."

Paul snorted and tossed a piece of bacon to Max, who snatched it from the air and swallowed it whole. "You're supposed to take my side, Mom."

Kittie flipped a long, gray braid over her shoulder and her blue eyes—the same glass-blue as her son's—flickered with good humor. "There are no sides in a family circle. Now, speaking of taking sides, you better give Oscar a piece of bacon, too. No favorites."

They all glanced down at Oscar, the eighty-pound black mutt that Paul had pulled from a kill shelter and trained as a personal protection dog for Harper three years ago, after a six-year-old girl went missing from a neighboring town. Amelia Larson. They never did find her, even though they'd brought in help from the state police and FBI.

Oscar's long tongue was hanging from his wiry terrier-like beard, his pointed shepherd-like ears standing at alert; dark, intelligent eyes locked on Paul's plate.

"Sorry, Oscar." Paul picked a piece of bacon out of the syrup puddle on his plate and offered it to Oscar, who took it gently from his fingers. "Good boy." He glanced at Harper. "Okay, kiddo, why don't you go grab your bag, and we'll get this day of fun started."

The deep dimples Harper had inherited from Mila appeared as she began gathering up the dirty plates, blue eyes sparkling mischievously. "My choice this time." She carried them to the kitchen, then skipped toward the stairs. Oscar followed dutifully behind her.

"Don't forget your epi-pen," Mila called.

"Mom! I know!" An exasperated tone gave them a glimpse of her coming teenage years.

"I'm not taking her to a bee farm," Paul said teasingly.

"Bees are everywhere." Mila dropped her gaze and stabbed at her pancake, discouraging him from making some snarky comment about covering Harper in Bubble Wrap.

Paul picked up his coffee cup, seemed to get the hint and changed the subject. "Hurricane Henry is crossing Cuba tonight. Then we'll have a better idea what to expect. You want me to get the boys to bring sandbags?" "The boys" were two of his fellow K-9 officers, Jackson and Mateo, who had become more like brothers.

Mila sighed. Preparing for a hurricane was not something she wanted on her plate this week. "I'll let you know tomorrow." Henry was a Category One at the moment, expected to slow down as it crossed Cuba then regroup and strengthen as it turned toward Florida's west coast. Where exactly landfall would be was anyone's guess. The spaghetti models had landfall somewhere between Tampa and Tallahassee, so Edgewater was in the Cone of Uncertainty. Uncertainty was like fire ants gnawing on her nerves. She hated anything she couldn't plan for.

Her phone trilled from the kitchen, where it was plugged in and charging next to her grandmother's set of three colorful ceramic chickens. Her Grandma Mary had loved those chickens and had been so excited when they found them at Thrifty's Antiques, so Mila hadn't had the heart to move them. They were a nice daily reminder of her, anyway.

Kittie gave her a sympathetic half-smile. "So much for a day off."

"Maybe it's a telemarketer," Mila said, as she scooped up her plate and carried it to answer the call she had a feeling was definitely *not* a telemarketer.

Three

Mila knew exactly where the old lifeguard stand was. When she was a kid, it had been manned by a sun-kissed blonde named Shelly and her equally tanned, buff boyfriend Todd, until they'd graduated and gone off to God-knows-where. Mila and her older sister, Harper (her daughter's namesake), had studied them behind the cover of plastic sunglasses, fascinated by the flipping of hair, giggling and all the subtle touching. Those were good memories. Before Harper's schizophrenia changed all that.

What had happened to the young couple? Had they stayed together? Maybe they'd broken up but found each other again like one of those country music songs. Either way, as a cop, Mila had a front-row seat when love and infatuation grew into patterns of violence, pain and sometimes murder. These cases, along with her own failed marriage, had turned her into a hardened skeptic when it came to relationships.

Mila parked her white Chevy SUV—complete with blue Edgewater Police markings and flashers set in the grille and rear bumper—in the small strip of parking spaces, squeezing in beside the Medical Examiner's crime scene unit van. Then she made her way down the gray, wooden boardwalk between the sea oats swaying on both sides.

Normally, she would take a moment to greet the vast, glittering water and let it run over her bare feet. She'd acknowledge the breeze playing with her hair, and the sunlight warming her face. The beach was her church, where she felt closer to some power greater than herself and less alone. But today she trudged through the sand in her rubber-soled, sensible black shoes, toward the activity and the body. The thin screech of seagulls hit a raw nerve. She took in a deep breath of the salty air through her nose, out through her mouth to prepare for what she was about to see. It never got easier.

This stretch of the beach used to be more popular when there was direct access from an off-road parking lot. That parking lot had been turned into a Senior Center years ago, so access to this beach was a good quarter of a mile north. People were more likely to congregate in front of the beach access points instead of carting blankets, coolers and beach chairs a quarter mile through hot sand.

She walked up to the edge of the yellow crime scene tape and stood beside Detective Frank Sartori, who was watching Sergeant Lockett. The sergeant was positioned in front of the lifeguard stand, motioning to one of his inexperienced officers. Frank had his hands shoved in his slacks pockets, his gray hair shorn in a fresh, spiked cut, his glasses darkened from the sun, and sweat was beading on his forehead. It was already close to eighty-five degrees with clear turquoise skies; no sign of the impending hurricane.

"Hey, Frank." Mila glanced up. Five large buzzards drew lazy circles in the sky above them. "What have we got?"

"A goddamn waste of a young life." He didn't look at her. He'd been moody lately, distracted. Probably because of his current divorce negotiations with wife number three. When Mila didn't respond, he sighed. "Girl, early twenties, slit wrists. CSU says it looks like a suicide. Dr. Singh will know more when she gets the body back to the morgue for examination."

Mila's chest constricted at the word *suicide*.

Rain rolling off black umbrellas. The sound of her mother's quiet sobs beneath the preacher's reading of the Bible. Her dad like a stone statue beside her mother. The sickly-sweet smell of wet flowers.

She shoved away the images of her sister's funeral and silently assessed the scene.

Six uniforms, their radio chatter joining the shrill cries of seagulls. Most of them Mila knew well from her patrol days. She waved at Officer Barb Polanski. Her thick, black hair was pulled back in a bun, a grim expression on her face as she stood, holding a logbook, in front of a strip of red crime scene tape in the "hot zone" closer to the lifeguard stand.

Another familiar tech, Brooklyn Lange, wearing a gray polo with "Medical Examiner" in block letters on the back, clad in paper booties and gloves was kneeling, snapping photos of the area beneath the lifeguard stand.

Mila's attention moved to the couple and their dog down by the shoreline. "Have you talked to the person who called it in yet? That them?"

Frank followed her gaze. "Polanski said their dog alerted them to the body. I got her notes, but I haven't talked to 'em yet if you want to do the honors."

Mila glanced over at Frank. Usually, he was on the ball getting witness statements. Something was definitely going on with him, but now wasn't the time to ask.

The wind molded her blue polo with the Edgewater PD logo to her torso and blew sea spray mist in her face as she approached the couple. She appreciated the respite from the heat.

"Hi, I'm Detective Harlow. I understand that must have been pretty shocking for you, and I'm sure you'd like to go home. I just need to ask you a few questions and then you're free to go." She scratched the dog's ears as he approached her, muzzle and paws wet from digging in the surf.

"Benny Jones." The man held out his hand. Mila shook it, caught a faint whiff of body odor and whiskey from his sweating pores. "And this is my girl, Crystal. Crystal Deevers."

"Hello, Crystal." Mila opened her leather notebook and jotted down their names on a fresh yellow page. Then got their pertinent contact information.

"And that's Rojo." Crystal stared down at her dog, her face ghost-white, her voice void of inflection.

Mila nodded. "I understand he led you to find the body?"

"Yeah," Benny said. "Was barkin' his fool head off. Digging at something underneath the stand, and so I thought maybe an animal was in distress or died up there. Went and checked and holy mother of God… that's a lot of blood. I ain't never seen a dead body before."

"And you called 911 right away?"

"I did—" Crystal said.

"Yeah, yeah, I told Crys to call soon as I saw. I didn't bring my phone with me."

Mila immediately caught the power dynamic between them and didn't like it. She automatically scanned for bruises as she addressed Crystal. "Did you see anyone else in the area?"

Crystal opened her mouth to answer but Benny cut in. "Nope. Not a soul around."

Mila turned a hard gaze on Benny, waited until he showed discomfort then said, "I was asking Ms. Deevers."

Benny's brows shot up over his Ray Bans and he held up his hands. "Sure." Then he turned to Crystal. "Answer the lady."

Crystal was staring at Mila, her head tilted, a slight look of surprise and maybe gratitude lifting the corner of her mouth. She straightened her shoulders. "As Benny said, there was no one around. Which is why I bring Rojo here every morning. Let him run a bit." Then she glared at her boyfriend, a new hardness like a wet pebble in her bloodshot eyes. "Life is too damn short. You need to move out."

Benny sputtered and turned red as Crystal pulled Rojo closer to her. "Can I go now, Detective?"

Surprise surprise. Mila smiled slightly and gave her an encouraging nod. "Sure. I have your number if I have any more questions." She pulled out a card and handed it to her. "And call me anytime if you need *anything*." She gave Benny a hard stare as Crystal thanked her and walked away. Benny ducked his head and stumbled after her.

Mila watched their progress down the beach, Benny trailing behind Crystal, arms flailing dramatically while she completely ignored him. "Good luck," she whispered as she headed back to the scene.

Four

A second ME tech, P.J. O'Malley, a spindly woman in her fifties, dressed in the gray polo, her ID in a lanyard around her neck, made her way gingerly down the rotted steps and trudged their way through the sand.

"Detectives," she greeted them with a somber nod. Her long, red hair was still tucked up in a hair net, her face—heavily freckled from years of sun exposure—was set in an unusual show of sadness. "Y'all can go on up. Rhodes will fill you in on what we found so far." Despite being in Florida for thirty-six years, her Georgia accent was still strong, especially when she was upset.

"Suicide?" Frank asked.

Her freckled forehead crinkled. "Certainly looks that way. But Dr. Singh will need to examine the wounds. Hard to tell right now. Anyway, she should be here soon. Hopefully, she can give y'all a time of death." She glanced over at Mila with watery eyes. "Damn shame. She looks a lot like my kid." Then she walked off slowly, lost in thought.

Mila was a little shook by P.J.'s reaction and tried to prepare herself for what they were about to see as they signed Officer Polanski's logbook with their names and badge numbers, and then ducked under the red tape. The sand beneath the lifeguard stand, which Brooklyn had finished photographing, caught Mila's attention. It was disturbed where the dog must've dug at a large dark, dried area. *Blood.*

The cuts must be deep. If it was suicide, this was no cry for attention, this was a woman determined to leave this world.

Despite Mila's best efforts, the world fell away as her mind dragged her back to the day she'd learned her older sister had lost her battle with schizophrenia and taken her own life at nineteen. The grief had been as sharp as knives, slicing her heart into pieces. She still missed her big sister every day. It had seemed unsurvivable, but here she was.

Mila forced herself back to the present moment as they approached Sergeant Lockett.

"How you doin', Frank? Mila?" he asked, hands resting on his hips, bald, brown head glistening with sweat. She'd loved working under him on patrol because he always expected more than she thought she could give. Always pushed her to be her best self.

"Good, Sergeant," she answered with a professional nod. "You can dismiss your uniforms, except for Polanski and Sanchez. And I guess Meyers needs the experience. Ask them to widen the search area to the parking lot."

He squinted down the beach. "Agreed. There isn't likely going to be a crowd here to fend off, and the less uniforms, the less opportunity for contamination." He glanced meaningfully at her and then Frank. "Let's get a bow on this one quickly, all right?"

"Yes, sir," they said in unison.

Mila and Frank slipped on paper booties, hairnets and purple Nitrile gloves and made their way up the stairs. They really should be using disposable, full-body Tyvek suits, but that expense wasn't in the budget. One downside of a small-town police department.

"Jesus," Frank muttered under his breath as they paused in the doorway to take in the scene.

The coppery smell of blood was strong, along with the underlying scent of decay. Fat flies buzzed around the body. Mila's heart began to race, a wave of dizziness overtaking her as an image of Sabine lying in bloody sheets flashed in her mind. In a daze, she reached up and touched the scar that ran from her jawline down to her collarbone. When she realized what she was doing, she dropped her hand and took a deep breath in through her nose, pushing away that fateful night with a hard shove.

Hands trembling, she glanced at Frank, making sure he hadn't noticed. He was too focused on the body, thank God. She'd learned the hard way, any whiff of weakness would be picked at by him like a vulture digging into fresh meat. She'd stopped taking it personally. It was just the way he worked. It didn't make him any friends, but it did make him a damn good detective.

The young woman was lying on her back on the weathered, wood-planked floor, thin arms by her sides. Each arm had a wound starting at the wrist and running all the way up to the crease in her elbow. Blood had congealed in the wounds and on both sides of her body into sticky black puddles. Her hands were already encased in paper bags to preserve any evidence. Her face was alabaster, eyes open, corneas clouded, and long blonde hair with purple streaks fanned out like a halo. She was wearing pink cotton shorts and a gray T-shirt with two cartoon frogs kissing. There were also cuts on her pale thighs.

Two yellow evidence markers had been placed beside her body.

Rhodes, the third ME forensic tech was in the corner, camera hanging against his ample gut, a sketchbook and pencil gripped in his gloved hand. He greeted them with a shake of his head, eyes dark and unreadable behind black-framed glasses. "It's a bad one."

"Yeah," Mila agreed, wondering if this case would nudge him toward the retirement he'd been talking about lately. Their quiet little coastal town didn't usually see violence to this degree, whether it was self-inflicted or not. She opened her notebook. "Did you find the weapon?"

"We did." He picked up a paper evidence bag from a box in the corner and handed it to her. "Marker one is where we found it."

She glanced at the yellow plastic evidence marker, "marker one," beside the victim's right hand, then reached in with her gloved hand and lifted the item, held it up so Frank could see it, too. It was a pearl-handled penknife on a keychain with two copper keys and a sparkly, red, stained-glass heart with the name "Rose" in white. The one-inch blade was open and had traces of blood in the indented channel.

Mila returned her attention to the gaping wounds along the woman's arms. "She did that with this?"

Rhodes shrugged, his expression unsure. "Her or someone else. The cuts may be too deep to be self-inflicted, but it's sure staged like a suicide."

Frank had moved closer to Mila to observe the keychain. "Looks like her first name may be Rose. Any ID?"

"Nope. We did find this." Rhodes pulled out a larger paper evidence bag from the box and handed it to Frank.

Frank lifted the item halfway out. "Brea Chardonnay. It's empty. Looks like she drank it for liquid courage. That would be consistent with a suicide."

Mila gave him a sharp look. He knew better than to jump to conclusions, to form an opinion and then try to fit the evidence to that opinion. She had to make sure whatever was going on with him wouldn't interfere with the investigation.

"Marker two is where the bottle was found," Rhodes offered.

Mila let her gaze roam the area. Something bothered her, but she didn't know what yet. She had learned to not just consider the evidence at the crime scene, but what was missing. What was missing so far was an ID for the victim. No purse, no wallet.

Does that mean a robbery?

Also, no suicide note, though that wasn't unusual. Most victims didn't leave one. And the third thing was no evidence someone else was here. Would a killer have been able to avoid all the blood? Leave it undisturbed? Possibly. If he or she stood where Mila was standing, in front of the small, dirty window next to the stairs and watched her bleed out.

"We should hold that conclusion of suicide until we know who she is and what her motive would be to take her own life." She moved to the victim's left side, careful not to step in the congealed blood and kneeled for a closer look. Waving her hand, she chased away the flies, their buzzing growing in volume. There didn't seem to be any hesitation cuts on her wrists that you see with a lot of suicides, though, again, it was hard to tell with all the blood.

There was a purple and black butterfly tattoo, about the size of a deck of cards, on the inside of her right bicep. That would make IDing her easier. *But the cuts on her legs? Did she start off by cutting and then decide to just go all the way? Was drinking a bottle of wine a factor in that decision?* She jotted down her observations then said, "Let's roll her over."

Wordlessly, Frank joined her, kneeling down and sliding his gloved hands under the victim's thighs. Mila slid her hands under the upper back and together they rolled the victim on her side.

She lifted the woman's shirt. A dark, purplish discoloration covered her backside, except where her body made contact with the floor. The flesh on her shoulder blades and backs of her calves were pale, where the pressure kept stagnant blood from pooling. She would've bled out until her heart stopped pumping, which was probably pretty quickly with those deep cuts.

"Can you grab some photos?" she asked Rhodes.

"Sure thing." He walked around and kneeled, the flash going off as he captured the pattern of lividity.

They rolled the victim back to her original position.

"She died here, wasn't moved. No bruising anywhere, no signs of struggle," Frank said, his voice low like he was thinking out loud.

They both stood and thanked Rhodes, then made their way back down the dodgy steps, and out into the fresh air. The contrast from death to sunshine was jarring. Mila balanced herself on the handrail to remove her booties, then pulled the hair net off as the sun warmed her crown quickly. As they removed the gloves from their sweaty hands, Mila said, "I didn't see a car key on that keychain. She must have walked here."

Frank opened a small trash bag so she could dispose of her P.P.E items. "Or got a ride?"

"Maybe." They exited beneath the second barrier of yellow crime scene tape. "We have to find out who she is asap."

"Detectives." Myers, one of the canvassing uniforms approached, his radio clutched in his hand. "We just got a call from a woman who says she was babysitting for a friend named Cara Anderson and Ms. Anderson never came home last night." He tore a piece of paper from a small notepad and handed it to Frank. "Could be nothing, but here's the address if you want to talk to her."

"Thanks," Frank said. "Any luck on finding a wallet? Purse?"

Myers shook his head. He was tall and tan, blond hair in a crew cut, twenty-four years old. Eighteen months of patrol without a training officer under his belt. Just a baby. He looked a little peaked. Mila wondered if this was his first body. "Not yet, sorry."

Frank turned to Mila. "You want to talk to the babysitter? I'll stick around, see if the canvas turns up anything and wait for Dr. Singh."

"Sure." She knew Frank was thinking this Cara Anderson wasn't the woman they were looking for because of the name "Rose" on the keychain and didn't want to waste his time. He'd also made it clear he was leaning toward suicide, which was wishful thinking. A suicide case would close a hell of a lot quicker than a homicide. She took the paper with the address and headed back to her car.

Elly Prescott, investigative reporter for the Suncoast Times appeared on the boardwalk heading toward Mila. "Detective!" She waved, her small frame decked out in black slacks and a bright orange shirt, glossy blonde hair blowing in the wind like a shampoo commercial.

Mila groaned. Elly was young, tenacious and hungry for a Pulitzer. The Suncoast Times had gone digital so her articles were posted quicker than Captain Bartol could put out the fires Elly started. The paper had also set up breaking news alerts so residents could sign up to get notified immediately when something important happened in the community. That was usually things like car accidents, new theatre shows or when aerial mosquito control would be spraying. A dead body on their beaches would be a shocking story that would get everyone talking... and demanding answers.

Elly struggled to keep up with Mila as she held a recorder up to her face. "Since you're here, I'm assuming this is a homicide? Can you tell me how she died?"

Mila knew Elly was baiting her. The reporter didn't even know for sure if the victim was male or female. She walked faster.

As she pressed the fob to unlock her SUV, she reminded herself to be polite. Turning with a forced smile, she said, "I don't have anything for you, Miss Prescott. I'm sure Captain

Bartol will put out a statement as soon as she can." Her smile dropped as soon as the door shut in Elly's face.

Everybody seemed to fall to Elly's charm, but for some reason the woman just rubbed her the wrong way. Mila had already searched her soul for the reason. She wasn't jealous, and she didn't have a problem with a reporter doing their job, as long as they didn't reveal sensitive information that would impede her investigation, which Elly would do in a heartbeat. She understood when a violent death occurs in the place people called home, it's reasonable for people to be invested, curious and concerned about that. But Elly Prescott seemed to thrive on notoriety instead of the story. It was Elly's motives that Mila didn't like.

That thought brought her back to the body in the lifeguard stand. If this wasn't a suicide, what would be the motive for someone to kill this young woman?

Five

Lotus Lane was the kind of established neighborhood street where the homes, built in the early 1940s, could be described as *darling* or *quaint* or *"beach cottage."* In other words, tiny cracker box houses with tropical-colored siding. The charm of the neighborhood couldn't be denied with its mature landscaping of palm and magnolia trees, huge birds of paradise and other flowering bushes that allowed something to bloom all year long. She liked to drive through with her windows down, enjoying the sweet scent of the flowering plants.

Mila especially enjoyed driving through the area after nightfall. Residents had recently started decorating chandeliers with various ornaments and beads, and strings of battery-powered fairy or Christmas lights, which they then hung from the live oak trees. The effect after dark, when the decorated chandeliers blinked and sparkled in the front yards, was magical and the trend had spread quickly around the block.

Mila pulled into the driveway of a small aqua-blue house. When she got out of the SUV, a racket above caught her attention. She shielded her eyes with her hand. Crows. Dozens of them flew around chaotically, cawing like they were all trying to talk at once. She didn't know how they avoided slamming into one another. Normally they would all be resting in the oak trees. Must be the approaching hurricane riling them up. With all their apps and radar, humans could never beat the animal kingdom for disaster early warning time.

She walked around the front enclosed porch, with open jalousie windows, to the side door beneath a metal awning and stepped up the two cement stairs. Before she could knock, the door flew open and a forty-something woman with coppery tresses and makeup smeared beneath her warm, brown eyes stood there. A baby girl in a pink shirt with butterflies and a tear-streaked, blotchy face was perched on her ample hip. "You're the police?"

Mila turned so the woman could see the badge clipped to her belt. "Detective Mila Harlow."

"Oh, thank the Lord Jesus. Come in." She stepped back and bounced the baby, who was starting to whimper. "Have a seat," she called behind her. "I'm just going to see if I can get something to occupy Rose."

So, Rose was the baby's name.

Mila took in the eclectic living space, mismatched, threadbare furniture and moving boxes piled up against the back sliding glass door. There was a speaker on the kitchen counter playing soft worship music. She made her way around the furniture to a group of framed photos hanging on the wall near a squat hallway.

Her heart sank as she stared at the young mother in the photo, the woman caught in a moment of laughter as her daughter gripped her purple-streaked blonde hair in a tiny fist. The butterfly tattoo was visible on her inner forearm. This was her. Cara Anderson. Once so alive and happy. *What happened?* She moved to the next photo: a closeup of Cara kissing her daughter's cheek, the little girl's gummy smile lighting up her face beneath soft, brown curls. Cara would never see her baby girl's smile again.

Mila had laid awake many nights after Harper was born, imagining all the ways her job could take her away from the new, fragile life she'd brought into the world. Fighting anxiety attacks as she'd imagine Harper growing up without a mother. That nightmare had become a reality for this little girl. She turned away as a lump formed in her throat.

The woman returned with a fussy Rose, holding a box of Cheerios in her other hand. "My name is Fayth, by the way. Fayth Gandy." She sat Rose on a blanket and then sprinkled the Cheerios in front of her. "That should keep her busy for a few minutes."

Mila moved some folded baby clothes from a sofa cushion and took a seat, then glanced down at Rose. The curls around her face were darkened with sweat, and wide brown eyes watched Mila back, a shiny bit of drool hanging from her cupid-bow mouth. Mila couldn't see the resemblance with her mother. "How old is Rose?"

"She just turned six months." Fayth rubbed both hands on her pale-yellow stretchy pants, plastic bangle bracelets clinking as they slid down her wrists. "I watch her for Cara once in a while when she has errands to run, but she's never stayed out overnight. She also forgot her cell phone in her purse in the bedroom, so I can't get ahold of her." She kept her eyes on Rose as the baby began to rock forward and reach for the cereal with a pudgy hand.

Mila frowned. *She left her purse here?* At least they knew it wasn't a robbery. Also, unusual for a twenty-something woman to leave her cell phone behind. Unless she knew she wouldn't need it anymore. "Leaving her purse and cell phone at home, was that something she did often?"

"Honestly, she wasn't attached to her phone like most twenty-somethings, so I'm not sure. I never had a reason to try to call her before while watching Rose." She shifted on the sofa to turn more toward Mila. "I know they say not to call in someone's missing until twenty-four hours, right? But I'm worried. This just isn't like her. She wouldn't leave her daughter all night."

"No, you did the right thing." Mila opened her leather notepad to a fresh yellow sheet. "So, no husband? Boyfriend? She lives here alone?"

"Yeah. She's not seeing anyone that I know of. Her whole life is Rose... well, Rose and her art."

Seems if Cara did take her own life, it wasn't because of a bad relationship then. "What about Rose's father? Do you know his name?"

She shook her head. "Cara said the man didn't want anything to do with a baby. Told her to "get rid of it" so she didn't put his name on the birth certificate."

Mila jotted that down. "What time did Ms. Anderson leave the house last night?"

"It was around eight. She said she shouldn't be gone more than a couple hours. I don't even know where she was going... she didn't tell me. Just said, 'I'm finally getting what I came here for.' I fell asleep when the baby did around eleven. Honestly, I thought Cara would be home soon, so we were just cuddling on the couch, waiting for her. I never even put Rose in her crib. Then I panicked when I woke up and saw Cara hadn't come home all night."

Mila tapped her pen on the notepad, thinking. "Do you know what she meant by finally getting what she came here for?"

Fayth reached down and fixed Rose's shirt which had gotten twisted around her belly. "No idea. We know each other from church, but you know... people are busy, we don't have deep conversations. Plus, she only just moved to Edgewater about four months ago."

That explained the boxes. She hadn't unpacked fully yet. "So, no other relatives here?"

"Nope. She's got an older sister, Charlie. Cara said she lives in Miami with her husband."

"Last name?"

"Yeah, it's Roosevelt. I remembered it 'cause it's like the president."

"What about friends, besides you? Anyone else she's close with?"

"Well, there's Jemma Burns. She's a bit younger than Cara, nineteen I think, but she watches Rose when Cara's working at the Farmer's Market. And Stew. Stew Prescott. He's got a booth at the Farmer's Market next to Cara's. Sells homemade jams. His cherry-chocolate jam is like crack. They hang out."

"Not romantically, though?"

"No, Stew's got a serious boyfriend. Plus he's like fifty-something."

Kittie had brought home some of that cherry-chocolate jam from the Farmer's Market more than once. Fayth's right, it is like crack. "And you said Ms. Anderson is an artist? Is that what she sells at the Farmer's Market? Her artwork?"

"Yeah. She creates beach scenes in wood frames, uses crushed sea glass, shells, dried starfish. They sell well at the market... you can check out some she's working on there on the front porch." She pointed behind Mila.

"I will, thanks." Someone's art could give an indication of their state of mind. "Does she rent or own this place?"

"Pretty sure she rents."

She'd have to contact the homeowner. "How did she seem to you last night?"

"You mean like... her mood?"

Mila nodded.

Fayth's mouth turned up at one corner and her eyes focused on the window behind Mila for a moment. Then she shrugged. "Fine. Happy, actually. She danced around the living room with Rose, both of them giggling, then she blew her a kiss before she went out the door."

That didn't mean much. Sometimes just the relief of making the decision to end the pain can make the person seem calmer and happier. "Was this her normal mood lately?"

Fayth seemed to catch on to Mila's line of questioning. "She wasn't depressed if that's what you're asking. But, no, she wasn't always that cheerful, either."

"Did she take a bottle of wine with her?"

"No."

She didn't have her purse. No ID or debit card to buy wine. Unless she had those in her pocket, but her pockets had been empty when they checked. "Any heightened anxiety? Withdrawal? Changes in her appearance?"

"I did see medication for anxiety in the bathroom. But no, nothing that would lead me to worry about her... disappearing from her life."

"Okay." Mila nodded. "And did someone pick her up last night? An Uber? Cab?"

Rose was done with the Cheerios and had now crawled over to pull herself up on Fayth's knee. Fayth reached down and hauled the baby onto her lap. Rose reached for the white plastic beads on Fayth's necklace with a slobbery fist. "Nope. Rode her bike, like always. She didn't have a car."

Ah. Mila had noticed a green beach bike lying on the grass at the other side of the small beach parking lot. It would have been about a ten-minute bike ride to the beach from here. She asked Fayth for a description. It matched. She texted Frank to pick it up. Now the hard part.

She leaned forward and made sure she had Fayth's attention. "Miss Gandy, I'm afraid I have some difficult news."

Fayth's brows pressed down in confusion. Her thick lashes blinking rapidly. "Yes?"

"We got a call this morning about a deceased female matching Ms. Anderson's description."

Fayth stopped breathing, her mouth opened in an O. Mila gave her a moment to process the news. Fayth's voice was barely a whisper as she asked, "Are you sure it's her?"

Mila indicated the wall behind her. "From those photos, yes, I'm sorry."

Fayth squeezed her eyes shut and shook her head. "My God..." she opened her eyes and looked down at Rose, who was shaking the necklace and babbling. "But what about her daughter?" The words came out on a sob. Tears spilled down her cheeks. "I can't believe this is happening."

"We'll need to get a hold of Ms. Anderson's sister. See if she's willing to become Rose's guardian. In the meantime, she'll be placed with child services."

A sound of grief escaped Fayth's throat as she pulled Rose into her bosom and hugged her. "I'm so sorry, baby girl."

Mila was sorry, too. Cara Anderson seemed like a caring mom from what little she'd learned. Now this baby girl would have to grow up without the love of her mother to support her. Hopefully the sister would be willing to step into that role.

Rose squirmed and pushed against Fayth's chest with her pudgy fists, letting out a squeal. Fayth wiped at the tears on her face and stared at Mila. "Was it suicide? Is that why you were asking about her moods? Honestly, that just wouldn't make a lick of sense."

"We don't know for sure yet. We'll know more after the medical examiner's findings." She closed her notebook. Mila would need to contact the landlord Cara was renting from, ask him not to touch anything inside until they decided if they would need to investigate Cara Anderson's death as something other than a suicide. She stared at Rose. Her heart ached as she tried to imagine Cara making the decision to leave her child willingly. Fayth didn't think it was suicide, and Mila's gut was saying the same thing. So, who would take the life of a young mother? Was it someone she knew? Someone she trusted? The clock had already started on that question.

Six

On the way to the police station, Mila noticed lines at the gas stations were already wrapping around the buildings. During the last major hurricane, the gas pumps in the whole area were empty forty-eight hours in advance of landfall. That made a late evacuation impossible... well, that and the parking lot that Interstate-75—one of only two major highways out of Florida—became all the way into Georgia. They had plenty of bottled water at home, but Kittie had agreed to brave the crowds at Publix to try to get Harper's other favorite storm staples: peanut butter and jelly, peanut M&M's, and chips and salsa.

Mila pulled into a parking spot at Edgewater Police Station, grabbed her leather messenger bag and pressed the key fob to lock the doors. The 32,000-square-foot building was eighteen years old but built to withstand 220-mile-per-hour winds with redundant backup systems, including a full campus generator. This case may require her to stay at the station, so she'd probably send Kittie and Harper to stay at Paul's place, which was further inland and not in a flood zone. Living a few hundred feet from the Gulf was amazing... until a hurricane came. Her grandmother had replaced the roof, fence and repaired flood damage many times over the last few decades. Mila had gotten lucky so far and only had one storm cause damage when a tree landed on the back fence. Hopefully that luck would hold with Henry.

Mila strode through the bullet-proof glass doors, her shoes squeaking on the polished granite floor. She nodded a greeting to Officers Gentry and Simms, who were heading out in a hurry. She noted the tension on their faces. One thing she didn't miss was hurricane prep as patrol. Trying to make sure the people in the mandatory evacuation zones actually evacuated, and answering calls of fights over water, toilet paper and generators. Then when the winds reached forty miles per hour and their families were secure, officers brought sleeping bags to the station to ride out the storm. As soon as it was clear, they would head out to check on the 911 callers they weren't able to help during the storm, assess damage, and rescue people from flood waters because people just *had* to get out and drive around.

"Afternoon, Detective," Francine, the front office administrator smiled as Mila approached the bulletproof window she worked behind. Just last week they'd had a small party to celebrate her twentieth anniversary at the station, and had all pitched in and bought Francine a massage and makeover from Zen Salon and Spa. She'd obviously used the gift, as her gray hair, normally worn up in a tight bun, was cut in a fresh bob at her earlobes.

"Afternoon, Francine. Love the new haircut."

Francine lifted a bony, aged hand and fluffed the top of her hair with a grin. "I feel like a new woman. I can't thank you all enough."

"You deserve it for putting up with us." Mila chuckled and swiped her badge to enter the secured door to the left which led to the inner workings of the department, then made her way down the hallway that led to the Investigations Division. She reached the bullpen, a large, fluorescent-lit room with dark gray walls, shelves full of colored binders, and five desks. Three of the desks were cluttered with large computer monitors, files, a phone and personal items. One desk was a spare that they all piled files onto, and one was clear and had been waiting for a new detective for three months now since Willy Jackson had retired. She wasn't sure what the hold-up was. Probably the budget. The rumor mill thought for sure Officer Dolan, a twelve-year veteran of the force, would be moved up as he'd requested, but that hadn't happened.

Frank's desk was against the right wall, catty-corner to hers. There were photos of his two adult sons and their families, a few half-empty water bottles and piles of files. He was there, on the phone, his back to the room.

Mila's desk was near the windows on the left. The Venetian blinds were open and sunlight streamed in, exposing floating dust motes. She shoved her bag into the bottom drawer after removing her leather notebook.

Detective Aiden Reyes's lanky figure appeared from the breakroom in the back, long fingers clutching a baggie of some homemade snack as usual, his shaggy brown hair in need of a cut. He was in his late forties, but except for a few strands of silver in his hair and laugh lines around his mouth, he looked ten years younger. Maybe there was something to the vegetarian lifestyle. Or maybe he just had good genes. During an overnight stakeout when they were first getting to know each other, Mila had learned his dad was Cuban, but his Roman nose and 6'3" height came from his Turkish-Greek mother. Aiden was married to a 5'4" blonde yoga instructor and they had three young girls with red hair. Genetics were weird.

He grabbed the swivel chair and pulled it up to hers. Deep-set brown eyes framed by dark lashes met hers. He held out the baggie. Granola with nuts and dried fruit. "Heard we caught a body." Empathy softened his words. "Was it her? Cara Anderson?"

Mila sighed and waved off the snack. "Yeah. There were photos in the home. It's her. She's got a six-month-old daughter. Rose."

"Shit." He scrubbed a hand over his face and blew out a deep breath. "Sartori says preliminary indicates suicide?"

Mila held his gaze. "At face value. I'll wait for the autopsy."

His head tilted. "Something not sitting right with you?"

Mila sank back into her chair with a sigh. "Maybe it's just hard to believe a woman would leave her six-month-old baby to fend for herself in this world."

He nodded and tossed a handful of granola in his mouth. After a few seconds of chewing he said, "But that happens. And worse."

Before Mila could answer, Captain Bartol entered the bullpen. "Good, you're back." She snapped her fingers at Frank, made a "wrap it up" motion with her hand when he glanced back at her.

Colette Bartol was a no-nonsense, curvy woman in her late fifties with a smoker's voice, even though she didn't smoke, and a dyed-red pixie cut, which currently was showing gray roots. She'd been Captain of the Investigative Division for eight years now and was well respected by the community she'd called home for the last thirty years.

She shoved a hand into her black slacks pocket and focused her attention on Mila. "What did you find out?"

Mila imagined the young mother's face in the silver frames on the wall again, the happiness sparkling in her eyes as she held her daughter. Her stomach tightened. "I made a positive ID with photos in the home. It's Cara Anderson."

Frank had moseyed over while Mila was talking. He stood beside Aiden, a large bottle of Tums clutched in his hand. He popped one in his mouth, then said, "On scene, Dr. Singh said best guess on time of death, based on liver temp and the body being in full rigor, sometime between nine last night and one a.m."

Mila opened her notepad, wrote that down and then briefed the team on all the pertinent information she'd learned from Fayth Gandy. Then added, "I've got the sister's full name, shouldn't be too hard to find her in Miami. See if she'll take custody of Rose."

Captain Bartol nodded curtly. "All right, you start with contacting the sister. Hopefully, she can catch a flight in soon, in case they close the Miami airport after Henry crosses Cuba tonight. Zansi is doing the autopsy at nine tomorrow morning. You can attend that as well. She's not a hundred percent on this being suicide." She turned to Frank. "I know you're still working those burglaries, but for now, get the homeowner on the phone and ask him not to enter the premises until we know exactly what happened."

Frank raised a brow. His skepticism didn't go unnoticed.

A hand went to her hip, her eyes blazed. She didn't like to be challenged. "Problem?"

Frank's jaw muscle jumped, a tell he wanted to say something but was biting his tongue. Mila realized he wasn't upset about being sidetracked from the burglaries. He wasn't willing to move off of suicide. "No, Captain."

"Good, then go find this other girl, Jemma, who babysits Rose. See if she knows anything." Captain Bartol glanced down at Aiden, who had abandoned his snack on Mila's desk and sat with his arms crossed. "After Mila calls the sister, you both go talk to the friend, the one with the booth next to our vic's at the Farmer's Market. See if he knows what she was doing on that beach last night."

The three detectives checked in with each other and nodded. There were no partners here, they were too small a division. So, they usually investigated things on their own unless it was a big crime like homicide... then it was all-hands-on-deck until the thing was solved.

Stew Prescott was a bear of a man with a large belly, neatly trimmed gray beard and mustache and a sparkle in his light gray eyes. That was, until Mila told him why they were there.

They were seated in a living room that was a mix of coastal and industrial décor. The house smelled like warm berries. Stew had sunk into a pillowy beige sofa and was dabbing his eyes with a Kleenex.

"This just doesn't seem real," he sniffed. He looked up at them, seated across from him on the matching beige loveseat. "How? Did she get hit on her bike? I told her once snowbird season came, traffic would be too bad to ride that thing around. We offered to help her get a car..." his words got lost in a choking sob. "Oh my God... Rose." His face fell into his palms and the grief poured out of him in extended wails.

A long-haired gray cat sauntered around the edge of the couch, hopped up gracefully beside the distraught man and nuzzled his hand. Stew reached out and stroked the cat's head, his sobs turning to sniffles.

Mila and Aiden shared a glance and she saw the sadness mirrored in Aiden's eyes. He cleared his throat. "Mr. Prescott, we're extremely sorry for the loss of your friend. What can you tell us about Cara's life lately? Had anything changed? Did she seem upset about anything?"

Stew stared at the beach wood coffee table between them, its surface covered in well-used candles; empty, stained coffee cups and a large blue, glass mermaid. "She... um... no. She didn't seem upset about anything. She was at her booth all day yesterday. She loved talking to the customers and was her usual chatty self." They leaned in to hear his soft words as tears streamed into his beard. His gaze suddenly snapped up. "Wait. Why? Why are you asking if she was upset? Oh my... did she... hurt herself?"

Mila held up a palm. "We don't know anything for sure yet. We're just trying to understand what was going on in her life lately."

He shook his head slowly. "Nothing out of the ordinary. Her life was Rose and her art. She is... was such a good mom."

"So, no relationship? She wasn't seeing anyone?" Aiden probed softly.

"No. She would've told me. I know it seems silly, but in the four months since I've known her, we've gotten close. She's like the little sister I never had. She's family. She and Rose come over to have dinner with us every Sunday." His eyes unfocused as he fought another wave of grief. Probably thinking of the empty chair at the table on Sundays now. That was one of the things that had hit Mila the hardest when they'd lost Harper. All the empty, silent spaces where she should've been.

Mila watched him closely. "You said 'us.' Who else lives here?"

Stew's gaze found hers. "Oh, Alex Tremble, my boyfriend. He's just out trying to find some hurricane supplies. He'll be back soon." He glanced toward the door hopefully.

Mila jotted down the name. "Anyone else Ms. Anderson hung out with? Had gotten close to?"

Stew scraped his teeth along his bottom lip. "She seemed to be getting close with Pastor Burns's daughter, Jemma, and the lady she met at church who helps her out sometimes with Rose. Fayth."

Mila clicked her pen, thought about what Fayth had told her about Cara saying she was finally getting what she came here for. "Do you know what brought her to Edgewater?"

"No." Stew blew his nose in the Kleenex. "She never said. I assumed just a fresh start, a smaller, safer place to raise Rose... she came from Tampa... as you know, this is a pretty artsy community."

So, she hadn't confided in Stew what she'd come here for, either. "The Market is only open on Saturdays during off-season. That was enough for her to live on?"

"I guess." His tone suggested he hadn't really thought about it before. He glanced up. "She sells her work online, too. On Etsy. Under Salty Sea Art."

Mila's phone vibrated on her belt as she made a note of that to look up later. She pulled it out and glanced at the number. "Excuse me. I have to take this."

"Detective Harlow," she answered as she stood and walked to the front door for privacy.

"Hi, this is Charlie Roosevelt returning your call."

Mila rubbed the spot between her brows where a tension headache was beginning. "Yes, thank you for calling me back. I'm afraid I have some difficult news about your sister Cara."

"Cara? What happened?" Her tone was sharp with fear.

Mila gripped the door frame, needing to steady herself and her voice. "Cara was found deceased this morning. I'm so sorry for your loss."

In the silence, Mila imagined the woman processing the news that comes like a punch in the gut, stealing your breath and splitting your life sharply into a *before* and *after*. She remembered the moment her mom had taken her out of school to tell her about Harper's suicide, destroying her sense of the world like a bomb. How every morning she'd wake up and have to face Harper's death all over again. How grief somehow made the beauty of the sunsets they used to watch together sharper, painful in its own right. Grief made everything sharper, and she was sure Charlie was feeling the deep, stabbing pain in her heart right now.

A small sob like a gasp confirmed this. After a few moments, Charlie managed to speak, though her voice was shaky and constricted with fresh heartache. "How? And Rose? Is she okay?"

"We're not one hundred percent positive how yet. There'll be an autopsy in the morning. But yes, Rose is fine. That's actually what I need to talk to you about. Rose is with social services right now, but ideally, it would be best if she was placed with family. Would you be willing to be Rose's guardian?"

"Of course. What do I need to do?"

A bit of relief loosened Mila's shoulders. "We need you to come to Edgewater as soon as you can."

"Done. I'll come straight to the police station when I get in tomorrow."

As they walked back to Mila's SUV, Aiden sighed. "Doesn't seem like we're uncovering anything in Ms. Anderson's life that would point to suicide, does it?"

Mila shook her head. "Hopefully the autopsy tomorrow will tell us something one way or the other."

Seven

Monday morning, Mila stood in her living room, clutching a warm mug of coffee and watching meteorologist Gina Hernandez gesture to the map of Florida on the TV screen, relaying the latest update from the Hurricane Center on Henry. The woman's bright pink blouse clashed with the angry red storm, its well-formed eye in the center, now churning between Cuba and the tip of Florida. Mila turned it up just enough to hear over Kittie's clinking in the kitchen as she made breakfast and sang to herself.

The meteorologist's tone was appropriately concerned but professional. "A hurricane warning is up for a portion of the west coast, as well as a tornado watch, and Henry is strengthening as expected. The center of the storm is sixty-five miles north of the Keys with gusts around 80 miles per hour. Later today Henry is expected to lift to the north northwest and begin to impact the west coast with landfall likely early Wednesday morning as a strong Category 1, which can produce a storm surge of six to eight feet."

Mila frowned. The house could handle a Cat 1 though she would still put the shutters up. The Hurricane Center didn't always get it right. She'd learned to hope for a Cat 1 and prepare for a Cat 5. She'd take Paul up on his offer of sandbags. At least in front of the garage.

The thump-thump of Harper skipping down the stairs, and Oscar's toenails clicking on the wood steps behind her, made Mila turn off the TV. Harper had inherited Mila's propensity for anxiety, so she didn't want her worrying about the storm yet.

"Good morning." She watched as Harper, wearing a blue, flowered cotton dress and white leggings, set the pet carrier she used when they traveled with her pet bearded dragon on the table by the front door, along with a grocery bag. Mila pasted on a smile and held her empty coffee cup out of the way as Harper wrapped her arms around Mila's waist. She stroked her daughter's soft hair, which was worn down for now, but there was a purple scrunchie on her wrist.

Oscar licked Mila's arm in greeting and then trotted into the kitchen to be let out into the backyard. Kittie, her gray hair in her signature two braids down her back, patted his head and opened the sliding door for him. Warm morning air wafted in as he trotted out into the fenced backyard.

Mila glanced down at her daughter. "Ready to have the best day ever?"

Harper scoffed playfully. "You say that every day." She looked up, her eyes bright with a good night's sleep, and Mila caught a whiff of strawberry-mint toothpaste. "How can every day be the best day ever?"

"You got me there, smartie. Maybe some days are just the second best ever." She kissed the top of Harper's head. "Besides I see you're taking Iggy to school today to share with the class. That's going to be fun."

Harper pulled away and bounced on her bare toes, her toenails sparkling with fresh glittery polish. She was such a contradiction. She loved all things glittery and girly but was obsessed with reptiles. "Yep. I've put some towels in there to keep him warm and have his lamp stand and basking rock if he gets too cold in the air conditioning. But I still don't think Iggy is going to think it's the best day ever since he's going to school." She twisted her mouth into mock disgust.

Mila knew Harper enjoyed school, both the learning and the friends, but she'd learned to pretend to dislike it to fit in. "I'm sure he'll love meeting all your friends."

"Breakfast!" Kittie sang from the kitchen.

"Coming!" Harper called back, imitating her grandma's upbeat tone. She tilted her chin and looked up at her mom. "What are you doing today to have the best day ever?"

Cara Anderson's body lying on a cold metal table popped into Mila's head. Her smile stiffened. "I'm going to get an extra hug from you." She pulled her daughter in and squeezed her until she started faking not being able to breathe and giggling again.

"There," Mila said, smoothing down Harper's hair where static had it standing on end. "Now let's go eat and then I'll drop you and Iggy off at school today."

What should've been a twenty-minute drive from Harper's school south down US-19 to the building which held the morgue and forensics lab, took forty minutes because of two major accidents and traffic backups around Walmart. The water and toilet paper shelves were probably bare by now. Also, anxiety would be running high and patience would be running low. Luckily Kittie had the patience of a saint and could handle being in the crowded, stressful environment. One more thing Mila was grateful for.

Her tires crunched gravel as she pulled into the parking lot on the side of the tan, two-story concrete building and made her way through the front glass doors. She approached Carmen, the thirty-something Latino woman who'd been a fixture at the reception window since Mila had been at Edgewater PD.

Carmen shot her a distracted smile and held up a finger as she finished a phone call. When she hung up, the corner of her mouth turned down. "Detective," she said, grabbing a visitor's badge. "Sorry you got the short straw on this one. I heard the victim is young and has a little girl."

Mila accepted the badge on a lanyard and slipped it over her head. "Yeah she does... did. Six-month-old baby named Rose. Speaking of babies, how's your little man?" Carmen had just come back from maternity leave and had the dark eye bags and swollen cleavage of a nursing mother.

Her puffy, hazel eyes welled up and she laughed. "He's amazing and I miss him every second I'm not with him." She waved her hand and wiped a tear from her cheek. "Sorry, I don't know what's wrong with me, I'm so emotional."

Mila smiled sympathetically. She remembered the emotional rollercoaster of being a new mother like it was yesterday. "Just hormones and lack of sleep. Hang it there, it calms down eventually. Got a photo?"

Her eyes lit up as she grinned. "You know I do."

Mila gushed over the cute little six-week-old and then Carmen buzzed her into the main hallway. She walked to the back, where electric doors slid open, and found herself in the cold morgue, the stench of formaldehyde and chilled meat assaulting her senses. She pressed the back of her hand to her nose, fighting to keep down Kittie's veggie scrambled eggs. Once the wave passed, she pulled a mask from a box on the shelf to her right.

"Morning, Detective." Dr. Zansi Singh stood beside Cara's corpse lying on the stainless-steel autopsy table, arms crossed over a blue surgical gown. Zansi was in her mid-fifties, black hair piled up in a bun, small frame straight, despite leaning over bodies for hours. And as always, her dark eyes radiated compassion and patience. Today, her eyes also smoldered with uncharacteristic anger. Her assistant, Chalondra "Lonnie" Robinson—who Zansi referred to as her "right hand"—perched on a step stool, taking close-up photos of Cara's forearm wounds. A paper sheet mercifully covered the rest of Cara's corpse.

Mila slipped her mask on and moved closer to the body, still not ready to give it her full attention. Instead she held eye contact with Zansi. "No good morning starts like this. Did you guys get anything from the clothing?"

"We did." Zansi turned to the table beside her and held up two sealed and labeled yellow envelopes. "Two hairs that were not hers. One has a root." She placed it back on the table with a gloved hand. "We already got her nail clipping, body fluid and swabs to send to the lab." She walked over to the large monitor, wiggled the mouse so it came to life, then used a pencil to point to the x-ray on the screen. "There are signs of previous trauma. This one is a broken and healed wrist." She tapped the keyboard and the image changed to a second ghostly gray and white image that Mila recognized as the spine and rib cage. Zansi pointed to a faint circle on the fourth rib down. "And this is a callus formation from a healed rib fracture."

Mila now knew why Zansi had a fire in her eyes. She was passionate about abused women and frequently participated in charity work for the cause. Along with losing her mother to domestic violence when she was twenty-two, she also lost a good friend a few years ago.

Mila allowed herself to look at Cara Anderson's face after Lonnie stepped gracefully down from the stool and acknowledged Mila with a nod.

Cara's eyes were milky, her skin bloated and tinged gray. Now that the gaping wounds in her forearms had been washed of clotted blood, Mila could see just how deep they went. Her gaze traveled down to the cuts on Cara's thighs and she squinted hard. "Wait... are those..." she leaned in closer, tilting her head. "Are those letters?"

Zansi nodded. "Yes." With a gloved finger, she traced above the left leg. "This looks like 'FORGIVE." She moved to the right thigh. "And on this leg is 'ME'."

"Forgive me?" Mila stared at the crude cuts in the bone-white flesh. "Is this her suicide note?" Something wasn't right. "No, these letters are upside down, like someone was at her feet when they carved them into her legs."

"Yes. Plus, if it was self-inflicted, she would have had to do that first and they would've bled more." Dr. Singh sighed. "The biggest problem is these wounds." She picked up Cara's right arm, cradled it in her gloved palms like a precious artifact. "These cuts match the penknife found at the scene, the depth inferring the blade was plunged in all the way to the hilt and dragged up the arm. There are no hesitation marks, no defensive wounds on her hands, no bruising to indicate struggle, no evidence that she fought someone."

Mila's head snapped up and she met the doctor's intense gaze. "This definitely wasn't a suicide."

Dr. Sing's delicate nostrils flared, dark brows pressed down. "No. The depth of the wound sliced through her median nerve and the flexor tendons from the flexor digitorum superficialis to the flexor carpi radialis. She would have had no motor functions in her wrist or hand, no way to grasp the knife to make the cut in the second arm. Someone else had to do it. She bled out in minutes so, if I don't find anything else during the exam or tox screen, official cause of death is going to be hypovolemia."

Even though it had been a possibility all along, the fact this young woman was murdered, that her life was cut short purposefully, felt like a physical blow to Mila's solar plexus. Stomach acid climbed up her throat as she fought the all-consuming rage threatening to blind her.

Deep breath in. Blow it out. The mask suctioned to her face, released. Suctioned, released. *Keep your perspective, Detective. You have a job to do here and that job does not involve your feelings.*

When she had successfully turned the rage down to a simmer and could speak calmly, she said, "Someone really wanted to make sure she didn't survive." Mila stared at Cara's face. Her last moments locked in a brain that no longer had electrical activity, could no longer tell its secrets. *What happened? Who did this to you? Did you know what was coming? Did you silently say goodbye to Rose? No, that would've meant you were conscious when someone did this to you.* All the things this woman had planned for her life, for her daughter. Now, she would never get to do them because someone decided they had the right to cut her life short.

"Let's find out if there's anything else Cara can tell us." Dr. Singh pulled her own mask on, folded down the sheet, exposing a fist-sized rose tattoo on the young woman's chest, right above her heart. She picked up a scalpel and began the internal postmortem by making a Y incision from the left shoulder, around the bottom of her breast to the lowest point of her breastbone, cutting through the tattoo as she sliced through skin then fat then muscle. As she peeled the skin away and exposed the ribs, Mila's mind reeled.

There was no way Cara had just laid there and let someone carve her up. She had to be incapacitated or unconscious.

She ran through a few scenarios in her mind and landed on her being drugged. "How fast do you think we can get prints back on the wine bottle and pen knife?"

Dr. Singh was using pruning shears to sever the ribs. "I'll see if I can get that expedited today now that we're looking at a definite homicide."

Mila moved her attention to the large metal bowls on the counter as her stomach grew queasy. "That'd be great, thanks."

The rest of the autopsy revealed no signs of internal trauma or sexual assault, which was a small blessing. There was wine in her stomach, so Dr. Singh said she would also try to get the drug and tox screen expedited to determine her blood alcohol level and if there were any other drugs in her system that could've been used to incapacitate her. Even if she'd drank the whole bottle of wine alone, that wouldn't have been enough to put her out while someone inflicted that much pain and damage to her body.

After the autopsy, Mila gratefully headed back to the station to fill in Captain Bartol and write up the affidavit to get a Mincey warrant to search Cara's phone and house. What she really wanted to do was take a shower and change clothes, but she knew the smell of death was in her nose, so that would do no good.

Back at her desk, she completed these steps, checked the time and headed to the conference room off the Captain's office. Aiden and Frank were already in there, looking serious while they stood close, deep in conversation. They both glanced up as she entered the room and then moved to take a seat.

Captain Bartol was right behind her. She walked to the whiteboard in the front of the small room and placed Cara Anderson's DMV photo at the top. Then turned to Mila. "What have we got?"

Mila pulled her attention away from Cara's photo, her bright smile and pink skin, still full of blood and life, and explained what they'd learned at the autopsy, how Cara wouldn't have been able to make the cut in the second arm with the nerves in the first severed. Someone else had to do it, but there was no sign of struggle or her fighting her assailant.

"That would mean she was incapacitated. Drugged," Frank said.

"Yeah and there were no needle marks, so whatever was used could've been in the wine," Mila said. "Dr. Singh is trying to get those lab results expedited along with the tox screen." She glanced at Captain Bartol. "I think we need to find out who her baby's father is and where he was last night. There's no name on the birth certificate according to the vic's friend Fayth, but we need to pull that and check. Her sister, Charlie, may know who the father is. She should arrive from Miami sometime today."

Captain Bartol wrote on the whiteboard: *Baby father??* And underlined it. "What else?"

Mila leaned forward in the chair, staring at Cara's photo on the whiteboard. "The thing that's bothering me is Cara came to Edgewater for a specific reason." Her gaze swept the group. "She told Fayth that night that she was finally getting what she came here for. We need to find out what she meant by that. What did she come to Edgewater for?"

"I'm sure she didn't come here to be murdered," Frank said with his signature sarcasm.

Mila ignored his unhelpful comment. "We need to see if there's any evidence in the house of who she may have been meeting. I already wrote up the affidavit for both her cellphone and the rental house."

Captain Bartol nodded. "All right, I'll contact the owner, see when he can meet you at the house for a search. Aiden and Frank, I want you two to go to Ms. Anderson's previous address in Tampa and talk to the neighbors. See if there were any problems, if they can give you any names of friends or acquaintances there. If anyone knows the father of that baby. I'll get Matt to also do background checks on Cara Anderson's known acquaintances here."

Matt Lee was a detective in his early forties. He had been in a bad car accident that had severed his spinal cord five years ago, which left him in a wheelchair. He hadn't wanted to retire so Captain Bartol worked hard to get grants to buy a forensic computer and send him to get certified in digital forensics. Mila hated to think of his tragedy as a blessing, but he seemed happy and was a natural researcher. His skills had saved their butts on many cases. She hoped this would be one of them.

Eight

Mila had forty-five minutes before Cara Anderson's landlord could meet her, so she stopped at The Pour House—her mom's coffee and muffin shop—located on Mango Avenue in The Historic Commons for a much-needed caffeine infusion.

The Historic Commons are the heart of downtown Edgewater. A five-block grid of restaurants, breweries, whimsical shops, a local museum, and the Farmer's Market, with brick sidewalks and bronze antique lantern-style light poles. In the center of the grid sits Manatee Park, a small grassy area for picnicking around the fountain. A large bronze sea turtle statue painted in tropical colors by a local artist graces the entrance to the park.

Another feature of downtown is the Pinellas bike trail, a forty-five-mile paved trail that runs right through the middle of it and brings in traffic to the restaurants and shops.

Mila and her sister had biked that trail together many times growing up, though they hadn't been allowed to venture more than five miles south. She would never let her daughter bike that far without an adult. The thought left her sad and feeling a little bit guilty. It couldn't be helped, though. She knew too much now.

The small coffee shop had pine floors, reclaimed from a torn-down beach mansion, floor-to-ceiling bookshelves and a large chandelier sparkling above the array of cozy tables. It was one of her favorite spots to hide and regroup. Besides books, the bookshelves held interesting items that Mila's mom, Patricia, had picked up on her travels. Patricia hadn't ever traveled until she'd divorced Mila's dad, Michael, twelve years ago and decided to fulfill her dream of opening this coffee shop, selling her healthier version of baked goods and using the profits for her adventures. Their marriage hadn't been the same after Harper's suicide, so it hadn't surprised Mila and her siblings, though they weren't sure exactly what had happened between their parents. They weren't really the type of family to talk about feelings.

Her mom was currently on a mountain retreat in Asheville, but Nettie Baker, the manager and her mom's best friend, greeted her with a toothy grin from behind the glass bakery counter. Her long dreads were piled on her head and wrapped in a gold and green silk scarf, and sunflower earrings dangled to her shoulders. "Good morning, darlin'. The usual?"

Mila eyed all the fresh baked protein muffins, walnut croissants, lemon biscuits and other various "healthy" options. Her stomach was still queasy from the autopsy, so she passed on food. "Sure, and let's add a large black coffee."

They talked about the impending hurricane as Nettie made Mila's vanilla oat milk Espresso. Mayor Sheila Starek strode in and approached Mila. Her energy was unusually anxious, her gray spiral curls wind-blown, her normal blouse and slacks replaced by beige overalls and a black T-shirt. Though, Mila wouldn't blame her for feeling frazzled. This was turning out to be a stressful week.

"Mayor." Mila gave her a respectful nod.

Sheila had been mayor of Edgewater for twelve years now because of her tireless work to keep the town affordable for residents without compromising their small beach town roots.

"Detective." Sheila's warm, honey-brown eyes bore into Mila's as she rested a hand on Mila's forearm. "Saw your SUV outside and thought I'd pop in and see if there's any updates on that poor gal found at the beach this morning? Colette hasn't returned my call yet."

"Yeah, the captain has her hands full. I'm sure she'll get back to you soon." Mila glanced around to make sure no one was listening and then leaned closer, catching a whiff of Sheila's floral shampoo. "I attended the autopsy this morning. This was definitely a homicide."

Sheila's hand pressed against her chest as she processed the news. She leaned against the glass counter like her body was suddenly too heavy to hold up. "She was young, right? What was her name?"

"Cara Anderson. She was twenty-two and had a six-month-old baby girl named Rose."

"Lord." Sheila's expression contracted with empathy. "What is this world coming to?" She shoved her hands in her overall pockets and straightened to her full 5'7" height. "Well, I have faith in your team to find whoever is responsible for that baby growin' up without a mama."

"Thanks." Mila just wished she shared the mayor's confidence.

Nettie greeted the mayor as she handed Mila two large to-go cups and a white bag. "If the forecast stays the same, everyone in The Commons is boarding up tomorrow evening, so if your mum asks, tell her not to worry herself."

"Will do." Mila peeked inside the bag. "What's this?"

"A banana protein muffin." She held up large palms. "Hey, I'm just following your mum's orders."

Mila smiled and rolled her eyes.

Nettie's deep laugh escaped her throat. "And she said don't roll your eyes."

Mila shook her head, but it was kind of nice her mom knew her so well. "Thanks, Nettie." After saying her goodbyes, she stepped outside and walked down to the corner where she knew she'd find Roadie at this time of day. Roadie had been hit by a drunk driver twelve years ago and got addicted to pain meds, which led to a heroin addiction. After he'd been busted in a drug sting two years ago, she'd tried to get Roadie in a program to get him off the streets and in a rehab program in Clearwater but had failed. So, for now she did what she could to keep him alive.

He had his arms wrapped around his knees, leaning against the wall, a worn baseball hat pulled over his eyes. Inside the hat, she knew he kept a small photo of his daughter, who he hadn't seen in ten years. His dirty canvas bag of meager belongings was propped under his legs.

Mila leaned down and touched his arm lightly so as not to startle him. "Hey, Roadie."

He pushed his hat up and looked at her with bloodshot eyes. His face was covered in grime and a straggly beard. "Hey, Detective."

Mila placed the muffin bag on the ground beside him and handed him the coffee. "You have plans to get to the shelter if Henry heads this way?"

He accepted the cup with a shaky hand. Taking a sip, he closed his eyes and sighed. "Oh yeah. The storm. Suppose I'm walking."

The utter defeat in his soft voice made her heart sink. She was losing this battle. "That won't be necessary. I'll have a patrol car pick you up tomorrow night. You gotta be clean, though. No drugs in the shelter." She squeezed his shoulder. "You take care."

Mila pulled up in front of the aqua-blue house once again, parking on the street this time. She didn't have to wait very long for the owner to roll up in a silver, late-model Cadillac. She shouldered her messenger bag and got out of her SUV. "Burton Tally?"

"Yes, ma'am." He offered her a weathered hand, adjusted his checkered golf cap and openly eyed her scar. "Such a shame about Cara. She was a good tenant."

Mila rested her hands on her utility belt. "She always paid rent on time?"

"Yep. I was skeptical on account of her being an artist and all. Not a very reliable source of income. But me and the Mrs. decided to give 'er a chance with her being a single mom. What's going to happen to her young'n?"

Mila handed him a copy of the printed warrant. "We're hoping Cara's sister will take custody of her."

She followed him as he shook his head sadly and unlocked the front door for her. "I'll wait in the car so as I can lock up when you're done."

The air conditioning was off. It was like walking into an oven. An oven that had been cooking diapers. She fought the gag reflex and got to work.

First the main bedroom. She struggled to slip on the gloves over her already damp palms then glanced around the room. The nightstand was piled with books, the romance kind with busty women in the arms of shirtless men on the covers. She flipped through them, making sure there were no hidden scraps of paper. Then went through Cara's purse and wallet. Her ID, a gift card to Publix, First Bank debit card and eight dollars in cash. She slipped the cell phone into an evidence bag. Then searched the nightstand drawers: more books, a reading light, some eye drops. The closet was mostly bare, just a few hanging T-shirts and two sundresses. No sign of a boyfriend staying there. Her laptop was on the bed, though. That could yield some important information. She'd write an amendment to the warrant for it, and take it to Matt.

There was only one small bathroom in the hallway. She checked the shower, beneath the sink, only female products. There was a second toothbrush, but it was a child's.

Mila had started brushing Harper's gums before she had teeth, too. Maybe they could get DNA off the toothbrush to help find the father. She'd take that with her. Also, in the medicine cabinet was what looked like a full bottle of Xanax with Cara's name on the prescription. She dumped the pills in her gloved palm and counted them. Only three were missing. Not enough to incapacitate her while someone carved her up. She poured them back into the bottle.

The baby's room only had a crib, changing table and small dresser with three drawers half-filled with baby clothes. Moving back into the living room, she opened the tops of the boxes piled against the sliding glass doors. More romance books and art supplies. On the small bar separating the kitchen and living room was a vase with crunchy, black roses. Mila plucked the card out of the plastic holder and read: Forgive Me.

Her already overheated skin prickled as the image of those same words carved in Cara's thighs flashed in her mind. There was no name on the card, but they'd come from Anne's Flower Shop. Easy enough to get a warrant for who'd sent them.

Could they catch a break so soon?

The kitchen was clean and smelled faintly of bleach. On the fridge were some magnets holding photos of Rose and a shopping list. She sighed as she glanced in the trash can, then got to work sifting through it. Nothing.

Changing gloves, she snapped some photos and video of the whole house and the unfinished artwork on the front patio. *Shame. Cara had been talented.* Then she stepped back outside and got more evidence bags from her SUV for the toothbrush, Xanax and flower card.

As Mr. Tally locked up the house, Mila said, "Cara's sister is supposed to arrive from Miami today. I'll give her your number. Hopefully she's willing to pack up Cara's belongings for you."

He rubbed his wiry, gray beard. "She's welcome to stay here if she needs to. Might be easier if she has the little girl. I'll put up the shutters for her if Henry is heading this way." He handed her the house key.

"Thanks. You're a good man." Mila accepted the key, though she wasn't sure it would be emotionally easier for Charlie to be here. "I'll let her know."

She decided to start canvasing the neighborhood. There was no answer at the house on the left, so she walked up to the house on the right and knocked. An elderly lady, dressed in beige cotton pants, a white sleeveless shirt and pink slippers answered. "Yes?" Her blue eyes were sharp and clear beneath a cloud of gray hair. A small-boned yellow cat was winding its way around her ankles. She reached down and scooped it up.

"Sorry to bother you, ma'am." Mila unclipped her badge and held it up. "Detective Harlow, Edgewater PD. I was wondering if I could ask you a few questions about your neighbor, Cara Anderson?"

"Oh, dear." One weathered hand with age spots rose to cover her neck, the other clutched the cat tighter against her chest. She studied Mila and her eyes widened. "I got an alert about a body found at the beach. Said it could be a suicide. That wasn't her, was it?"

Mila cursed under her breath at how news spread like wildfire through small towns. Especially this small town, where Elly Prescott was so skilled at batting her eyelashes at male uniforms for information. She'd bet her paycheck it was the rookie Myers who'd talked. "We're not sure if it was a suicide but yes, it was Ms. Anderson."

The woman's eyes narrowed like she suspected she wasn't being told the truth. "Well, I didn't know her very well. She kept to herself or was out, mostly. I got to meet that sweet little baby, Rose, though." The memory brought a soft smile to her thin, pale lips.

"Did you ever hear any arguing over there?"

She thought for a moment. "No, can't say I ever did."

"What about see any suspicious persons? Vehicles in the driveway?"

"You know." She stroked the cat's head with an arthritic hand. Its pale green eyes glared at Mila, like it was her fault it was being held captive. "I was in the bathroom late last night... around midnight is when my bladder usually wakes me up. And I thought I saw a flashlight out the window. So I turned out the bathroom light and peeked out the blinds. It was real dark, no moonlight, but I could've sworn I saw a person all in black, standing there on the side of Cara's house. I knocked hard on my window. It looked like the person ducked and ran. Could've been a shadow from the palm tree, I guess. I was half-asleep."

Mila took down her information and thanked her. Then she walked between the houses and checked the ground in front of the window on that side of the house. It was the window in Rose's nursery. There was a strip of degraded mulch along the side of the house meant for landscaping, one sad, lone bush near the front. She kneeled down. In the mixture of dusty mulch and sandy soil was a partial shoeprint. Someone had been standing here. Were they planning on breaking in? The blinds were cracked open, so they would have been able to see into the room, into the crib. The print was only a partial, so hard to tell size. It had a waffle tread at the toe and then diamonds beneath that. Maybe a sneaker? Maybe it was from Cara's shoe? It's plausible she walked around her own house. Mila called dispatch and asked for a CSU team.

While they were finishing up with the cast of the shoeprint and dusting the window for prints, Mila went back in the house to make sure there were no shoes that could possibly match the print. There were only two pairs of worn flip-flops by the door. She'd have to have them compare the print to the sneakers Cara had on when she was killed. Then she texted Paul and told him to go ahead with the sandbags in front of her garage. A call vibrated her phone in her hand as she hit send. Charlie had arrived at the police station.

Nine

Charlie Roosevelt was sitting at one of the round tables in the front lobby, a carry-on black suitcase by her chair, her fingers typing something furiously on her phone. She was waif-like, her wheat-colored hair cut in a short bob right below her ears, her light blue slacks and white silk button-down perfectly tailored for her body.

"Miss Roosevelt?" Mila held out her hand. "Detective Harlow. We spoke on the phone."

Charlie stood, the movement sending a puff of expensive perfume into the air, and slipped her small palm into Mila's grip. A large diamond ring poked Mila's finger. "Yes." Her hazel eyes were bloodshot. "I got here as soon as I could. Is there anything else you can tell me? You said there would be an autopsy this morning?"

"Please have a seat." Mila slid into a chair next to her and took out her notepad. Then she folded her hands and made eye contact with Charlie. "There's no easy way to say this. Your sister was a victim of homicide. Someone cut her wrists and she died from the blood loss."

Charlie's small mouth opened and then shut. "I don't understand... you're saying someone intentionally killed Cara?" She was shaking her head no. "Who would do that?"

"That's what we're going to find out. Did your sister have any enemies? Maybe Rose's father?" Mila pushed the box of Kleenex toward Charlie as the tears spilled down her cheeks.

Her voice trembled. "Joey Bingham. He and Cara had been on and off since she was sixteen. I know he was abusive but she kept giving him chances. If that bastard did this..."

Mila jotted that down. "Physically abusive?"

Cara's neck had flushed with anger. "Yes, and emotionally, as well."

Mila glanced up. "So he's Rose's father? Cara didn't put his name on the birth certificate."

"She didn't?" She pressed the Kleenex beneath her eyes and grew thoughtful. "I mean, I always assumed."

Mila made a note to remember to pull the birth certificate. "I haven't confirmed it yet, but her friend said she left the father's name blank."

"Oh." Uncertainty washed over her, tightening her features.

Mila noted a bit of irritation, also. Maybe that her sister hadn't confided in her? "Do you know why Cara moved to Edgewater?"

A helpless shrug. "She said it was a good place to sell her art and a safer place to raise Rose than Tampa."

All true. But not the reason. "Were you two close?"

"We were, until Rob and I got married and moved to Miami two years ago. We'd talk on the phone a few times a month, but the distance did make it hard to keep up with her."

Physical distance does turn into emotional distance. Mila had learned that the hard way. "And your parents?"

She shifted in the chair with a small head shake. "Both gone. Car accident. Three years ago now."

"I'm sorry for your loss." Mila closed her notebook. "I can take you to the house your sister was renting. The landlord said you could stay there. We'll call child services on the way, let them know you're in town."

She swallowed hard and twisted the diamond on her hand. "I'd like to see my sister, Detective."

Even with the distance of a screen, seeing a loved one in the morgue is brutal. Mila was glad they had other ways they used to identify bodies now so this was rarely necessary. Everyone deserved to remember their loved one flushed with life, eyes shining, still reaching for dreams and goals. Not the image of an empty, lifeless vessel burned in their mind. She didn't like funerals for this reason, either. But that wasn't up to her. Some people, like Charlie, needed that closure. And she wouldn't deny her that.

Afterwards, Mila sat with Charlie in a private room with comfy chairs and soft lighting, created just for this purpose, letting Charlie cry and talk about her sister. Eventually, the sobs subsided, and she sat with her head down, drained and distant.

Mila checked her phone. She'd ignored a few texts as she gave Charlie her full attention.

One was from her younger brother, Adam, who lived in Sarasota, asking if she wanted help putting up the hurricane shutters. She'd call him back later. The other was from Candice at Child Services. They had the paperwork ready and were expecting Charlie.

Mila rested a hand on Charlie's forearm to get her attention. The fragile woman looked up, dazed, hollow purple circles beneath her eyes. "When you're ready, we can head to Child Services. They have a few hours of paperwork for you to fill out." Mila said it with a slight smile, but unfortunately, it was probably true.

Charlie straightened her back and took a deep breath. "I'm ready."

Mila gave Charlie the key to Cara's rental house and her cell number when she dropped her off. "Call me when you're done, and I'll get a patrol unit to drive you and Rose to the house." Then she headed back to the station to write up an affidavit for the flower shop and give Matt Cara's laptop and cellphone. She'd already given the lab the Xanax bottle and toothbrush, with a request for DNA from Rose's toothbrush.

After sending the warrant request, she entered the report number into the National Center Information Center system, or NCIC for short, and looked up the boyfriend, Joey Bingham. He had a pretty long rap sheet for a twenty-five-year-old. The most recent was an assault and battery charge by the Tampa PD. Weird no arresting officer was named.

Mila plucked the receiver from her desk phone and called them. "Yes, hi, this is Detective Harlow with Edgewater PD. I need the Records Department, please."

After a brief hold, a voice said, "Records."

"Hi, this is Detective Harlow with Edgewater PD. I need to find out who the arresting officer was for Joey Bingham on March 5th of this year."

Mila left Officer Stanwick a message. Hopefully, he would return her call soon.

Anne's Flower Shop was in The Commons between the Book Attic and Sweet Scoops Ice Cream Shop, across the street from her mother's coffee shop.

As she stepped in, the heady, sweet smell of fresh flowers greeted her and flooded her with memories. *Prom. Friend's weddings. Her roommate's funeral. Her sister's funeral.* She shoved them to the corner of her brain as she greeted the willowy blonde teenager arranging flowers behind the counter. Summer was Anne Freemont's great-granddaughter. Anne was the original owner of the shop.

"Hey, Detective." Her youthful smile flashed over a handful of baby breaths. "Any sign of winds picking up out there?"

"Not yet." She pulled a printed copy of the signed warrant from her messenger bag and slid it across the counter. "I need to get a name from you."

Summer unfolded the sheet of paper, silver rings glinting on her fingers, short nails painted a sparkly pink and her shoulders sank. "Oh. Cara Anderson. The girl who died. I saw her in church with her baby a few times." She glanced up, obvious fear in her eyes. "Did she really commit suicide?"

Mila felt impatience prickling through her system. She gave her the standard line. "It's an ongoing investigation."

A visible shiver went through Summer. "If she didn't, I hope you catch 'em soon. All my friends are freaked out. Afraid to go anywhere alone in case... you know."

Mila put her impatience in check. Of course the community would be on edge right now. Especially young girls. And really, they had every right to be, though they didn't know that. "Being cautious right now isn't a bad idea." She softened her tone. "How about that name?"

"Oh, sorry." Summer's blonde ponytail swung as she turned back to the computer and typed in something, scrolled and then the printer clunked on behind her. Pivoting, she pulled the sheet from the top of the printer and handed it over the counter. "There you go. You think he had something to do with her death?"

Mila stared at the name and address on the delivery order. There was a niggling familiarity, but she couldn't place it. "Just following all leads at the moment." She tried to give the girl a reassuring smile but there was no denying a senseless woman's death and a hurricane coming made for an unsettling time. "Thanks and stay safe."

She slid into her SUV, the leather seat warmed by the sun, and typed the name into the Mobile Data Terminal. She immediately recognized the area on the map, the house they had just been to yesterday and now she remembered the name. Alex Tremble. Stew Prescott's boyfriend. She threw the transmission into drive and hit the gas.

Ten

Stew answered the door, face flushed, a "kiss the chef" apron straining against his belly. "Detective. Is there news about Cara?"

She glanced into the house behind him. "Not yet. I need to speak to Alex. Is he home?"

Stew's expression shifted into deeper worry lines, but he waved her in. "He's in the back garden. Have a seat and I'll grab him."

Mila walked around and looked at the photos on the bookshelf. Seemed like Alex was about ten years younger than Stew and a foot shorter, with a wiry frame and wore his brown hair shoulder-length. There were various photos of them with groups of friends and one with just Stew, Cara and Rose. Both Stew and Cara were smiling down at a grinning Rose.

The sliding glass door slid open, and Stew lumbered in, Alex behind him pulling off garden gloves. His hair was scraped back in a ponytail at the nape of his neck, his light eyes were already assessing Mila curiously.

She introduced herself. "I just have a few questions for you if you don't mind." Then she glanced at Stew. "You can stay."

Alex lowered himself onto the sofa, took out a handkerchief and wiped at the sweat on his face and neck. His face was flushed from the heat.

"Let me just turn down the burner," Stew mumbled, shooting Alex a worried glance before heading into the kitchen. When he returned, he took a seat next to Alex and reached for his hand. "What's this about?"

Mila extracted the flower shop receipt from her satchel and handed it to Alex across the coffee table. "This says you sent flowers to Cara Anderson two weeks before she was killed."

Alex's shoulders seemed to relax. "Well, yes. Is that a crime?"

Mila mirrored his smile. "No. But the note seems to be an apology. What happened between you two?"

Alex's gaze slid toward Stew, the heat blush on his face turning a deeper red. Stew slipped his hand from Alex's and turned toward him with a catch in his voice. "Alex? What is she talking about?"

Alex looked at Stew imploringly. "Please don't be mad. I just had a moment of weakness. It's just we used to have Sunday dinners after church to ourselves and I missed that. I missed you. And so I..." he lowered his head, "that last Sunday, when she didn't show up for dinner... that was my fault. I'd ask her at church that morning not to come. She was really hurt. We had a brief argument." He glanced back up. "I'm so sorry."

Stew's lips pursed and his nostrils flared. "How could you?"

Alex held up his hands, his eyes growing moist. "It was stupid... I was jealous and I realized that, that's why I sent her the apology flowers. I also called and told her she was always welcome here."

"But it's too late."

Mila watched their exchange. Alex seemed sincere, but it was too big a coincidence that the wording was exactly what had been carved into her thighs. "Alex, where were you Sunday evening between nine and midnight?"

Alex's face drained of color as his attention shifted to Mila. "Here. Home. Oh God, you don't think I had anything to do with Cara's death, do you? I mean... I admit I had a selfish moment, but I would never hurt Cara."

Mila looked to Stew for confirmation. He was obviously still fuming but he gave a nod of agreement. "We were both here all night."

Mila believed Alex, but she would still need to see if there were any witnesses to this argument at the church. Make sure it wasn't more serious than he was letting on. Also, see if any of the neighbors could confirm they were home all night. "What's the name of the church you all attend?"

"Gulf Shores Community Church on Lime Street," Alex answered. His shoulders had fallen, while Stew's posture was stiff and radiating anger. She was glad she wouldn't be around for the argument they were about to have.

Mila spoke with the neighbors, who could only confirm both Stew and Alex's cars were in the driveway when they came home from the pub at one a.m. Then she headed toward the church. Halfway there, she got a call from Kittie. Her heart rate rocketed as her thoughts flew to worst-case scenario: Harper injured, missing or worse. Her chest constricted and her vision blurred. She swiped the green circle to answer the call but couldn't get any words out.

"She's fine. Harper's fine." Luckily Kittie understood what was happening. As Mila blew out a breath, Kittie quickly told her why she was calling. "Just talked to Ms. Taylor when I picked Harper up. She had a pretty rough day at school. Apparently one of the boys said he set Iggy free at lunchtime. They all spent thirty minutes looking for him around the school with Harper in hysterics before the boy admitted he'd put Iggy in his backpack to take home."

Mila's face grew hot as she imagined Harper in that much distress and her emotions morphed from fear to anger. "Let me guess, Mason Beaumont?"

"Who else? Iggy seems fine but Harper is still upset. You want to video chat with her? I know you're working that girl's case and won't be home for a while."

What she wanted to do was hold her daughter and throttle Mason Beaumont. She glanced at the time. "You know what, let me see if I can swing by in a few hours. I'd rather see how she's doing in person."

Lime Street was an eclectic mix of homes and businesses. Mila parked on the street next to the white picket fence separating the church grounds from the sidewalk. She wasn't sure if anyone would be here on a Monday afternoon at… she checked her watch.. damn. Four o'clock already. This day was going too fast.

She made her way up the cracked asphalt driveway beside the church, which led to a parking lot in the back. Then up a set of wide, white stairs to double doors painted rustic red. Pulling on the brass handles, the church doors squeaked open. She stepped into the cool interior.

The entranceway had thin, faded red carpet and wood paneling. A guest book stood on a podium beside the door, and there were fake palm trees in the corners. It smelled faintly of mildew. She could see into the nave through opened French doors. Two rows of pews, a pulpit on a raised platform up front with an oversized lighted cross hanging behind it. She walked into the empty nave, unnerved by the absolute silence. Three tall stained-glass windows glowed to her right. She was drawn to them. As she stood admiring the way the sunlight lit up the intricate scene of Mary holding baby Jesus, the three wise men around them, and angels floating above them, a voice broke the silence too close behind her.

"Can I help you?"

Mila stiffened and turned. She sized up the man quickly: 6 feet tall, early fifties, neatly trimmed beard, mustache, wavy brown hair. Not a threat. He held out one of his hands, his gaze sweeping over her scar curiously. "Collin Burns. I'm the pastor here."

Mila was used to the scar being the first thing people saw, so she wasn't offended. She shook his offered hand, recognizing the last name Burns. Jemma's father? "Detective Harlow, Edgewater PD."

Coffee-colored eyes sparked with curiosity. "What brings you to our humble little church, Detective?"

She watched his expression carefully as she said, "Cara Anderson."

A deep sadness faded the spark of curiosity in his eyes, wiped the smile from his lips. "Ah." His head bowed and his eyes closed. "Cara." He spoke her name as a whisper of reverence. When he looked back up, his eyes were full of pain and glistening with tears. His reaction seemed extreme for one of his members he'd only known for four months. "My wife and I have been praying for her soul, but I fear it will do no good," he whispered harshly.

"Her soul?" Mila's brows shot up. "Don't you usually leave that kind of judgment up to God?"

He folded his hands and nodded. "We believe suicide is an unpardonable sin because there is no way to repent and confess that sin."

Mila kept her opinion to herself. *Other people's faith is not your business.* "What if she carved the words 'forgive me' into her body before she died? Would that be repentance enough?" As she watched the pastor's horrified reaction, she questioned her own motives for sharing that information. She knew it wasn't a suicide, so there was no point in telling him that. Worse, it was information they weren't releasing to the public. A mistake she wouldn't normally make. Maybe she just wanted him to consider the extremes people go to in the name of religion. Maybe she was just letting her anger over a young, dead mother cloud her judgment.

She reeled in her anger with effort. "What can you tell me about Cara?"

His face had paled, and he seemed to still be struggling with what she'd revealed, but he cleared his throat. "Well, she's only been with us a few months, but she was a bright light." His head rocked back and forth as he sighed. "Also, a troubled young woman. My wife is a counselor and Cara has been seeing her for about a month now." A darker shadow crossed his face.

Was that guilt? Regret? Anger?

Mila watched the confusion and grief playing out in his micro-expressions, even though he was trying to stay calm. She was having a hard time reading him. "I'd like to speak to your wife."

He was nodding but also struggling to pull himself out of his private thoughts. "Certainly. We live in the house out back. Come on, I'll take you."

As they stepped out into the warm afternoon sunshine, Mila asked Pastor Burns some standard questions. *How long had he been at this church?* Four years. *Did he witness the argument between Cara and Alex Tremble a few weeks ago?* No, he didn't. And he seemed surprised by the conflict. *Where was he last night?* He had gotten violently sick and passed out around eight o'clock. Probably food poisoning. His family can confirm.

There was a young man pushing a lawn mower into a garage beside the small house. Pastor Burns nodded his way. "That's Santos. Good kid. Hard worker. He's been with us for about a year and a half now. We have two other adopted children, Jemma and Julian. They're actually blood siblings, and have been with us for ten years. Jemma's out helping some elderly members of our congregation prepare for the storm, but you can meet Julian."

Mila stepped around a weed whacker that had been discarded in the middle of the path to the house. "Jemma and Cara were friends?"

Pastor Barnes motioned for her to go up the set of steps to the house before him. "They were becoming close, yes, which was funny because Jemma has a hard time making friends. Cara was special, though. So easy to talk to and really cared about people."

"Can I get the full names of all three children, please?" They paused on the porch while Mila wrote down their names as he spelled them.

He shifted on his feet, genuine concern seeping into his tone. "So, what's going to happen to Cara's little girl, Rose?"

"Cara's sister is willing to be her guardian. She's doing the paperwork as we speak."

His brows furrowed. "I didn't know she had a sister. She lives around here?"

"No. Miami."

"Ah. I see." He opened the door and called inside. "Lynnie?"

The house was cramped, even with minimal furniture. It was warm and smelled like someone was cooking chicken soup. An elderly man with sparse gray hair and a long nose, sat in a wheelchair in front of the window across from a teenager. A checkerboard rested on the fold-out table between them. "This is Lynnie's dad, Lionel." Pastor Burns raised his voice. "Lionel... this is Detective Harlow." The man held up a large hand and then went back to staring at the board. "And that's Julian." The teenager gave her a distracted smile and wave.

A small woman appeared from the back hallway, frizzy, brown hair brushing her shoulders, a stack of books in her arms. When she spotted Mila, she paused and glanced at her husband.

"This is Detective Harlow. She needs to talk to you about Cara," he said.

His wife nodded, her expression distraught as she set the books down on a table and held out a damp hand. "Jocelyn but everyone calls me Lynnie." Mila gave it a quick shake. "Please have a seat. Can I get you a water? Coffee?"

"No thank you." Mila chose the chair with the Afghan covering the back. She opened her notebook and clicked the pen.

Lynnie and Pastor Burns settled on the sofa and looked at her expectantly. Lynnie spoke first. "Cara was an amazing young woman... such a talented artist and loving mother. We didn't see any signs she was suicidal." Her cheeks were blushed with Rosacea, her eyes a watery blue. "Do you have any idea why she did this?"

"We haven't confirmed it was suicide." She watched for a reaction and wasn't disappointed when the woman's eyes widened in surprise. It seemed genuine. "Your husband said you've been counseling Cara for the past month. Was she worried about anything or anyone specifically?"

Lynnie's mouth twisted to one side, hands rubbing her thighs nervously. "She said she moved here to get away from an abusive relationship, but she didn't indicate she was afraid he was coming after her here. We hadn't really had time to dig into that relationship, so I don't know much about her past. She mostly was just struggling with being a single mom. She had some anxiety, some questions about her faith. Nothing that would point to her being so unhappy." She glanced up sharply. "If she did take her own life."

Mila scratched out some notes on the yellow pad then asked, "That was the only reason Cara said she moved here?"

Lynnie's expression was open and thoughtful. "Well, she did mention she liked the smaller town. Thought it would be a better place for Rose to grow up. I don't know why she picked Edgewater specifically. I know she doesn't have family here, and I don't think she knew anyone here before she moved."

Mila tapped the pen on her notebook in frustration. Cara hadn't even told her therapist the real reason she came here. *Why? What was the big secret? It couldn't just be that she was fleeing an abusive relationship.* "I'm finally getting what I came here for." That's what she had said.

"Do you know when Jemma will be back? I'd like to speak with her."

"Shouldn't be more than a few hours. She's helping the Artinos bring in their patio furniture. George turned eighty-four this year and he's finally slowing down." She chuckled to herself then joy flashed in her eyes. "Jemma's a smart girl, too. She's taking online classes, wants to be a nurse. We're really proud of her." Her gaze fell to her lap. "She's been such a blessing since the Lord never did bless us with children of our own."

Mila gave her obvious grief about that a moment of silence. Her phone buzzed on her belt. She checked the number. "I'm sorry, I have to take this. Give me a call when she's back please." She handed Lynnie her card.

"Detective Harlow," she answered as she stepped back outside into the stifling heat, shutting the door behind her.

"Detective. Officer Stanwick. You had a question for me about Joey Bingham's arrest?"

"Yes, thank you for returning my call. His ex-girlfriend has turned up as a homicide victim here in Edgewater. What can you tell me about him?"

"Let's see…" computer keys clacked in the background. "Looks like he's twenty-four, last arrest on May 5th was for assault and battery stemming from a bar fight. He's out on bail awaiting trial. Last year was a misdemeanor trespassing charge and another assault charge at eighteen."

None of those had anything to do with Cara Anderson. "No domestics?"

"None reported. Though it wouldn't surprise me."

"What's the address listed for him?"

He told her and she thanked him for his help. The address was different from Cara's previous address in Tampa. When had he moved?

Before she headed back to the station, there was something important she needed to do.

Eleven

Mila's Grandma Mary had two best friends in Edgewater who were still living, both in their late seventies, Ruby and Judith. They were like family. She needed to stop in and check on them, see if they had someone to put up their hurricane shutters.

Ruby still had a palm and tarot card reading business that she ran out of Seven Moons, a crystal and metaphysical shop located in the bottom floor of a Bed & Breakfast she also owned. The place smelled like incense and had soft, chanting music piped in the space. Ruby appeared from the back where she did Tarot card readings, pushing through the hanging beaded curtain with her signature wide smile and open arms.

"Mila! How are you, my darling." Her hug wrapped Mila in warmth, lemongrass and patchouli. A raw, rose quartz necklace pressed into Mila's chest.

Mila stepped back, squeezed Ruby's narrow shoulders and smiled into her heavily lined, onyx eyes. Her short, black hair was peeking out the sides of a red, silk head scarf. "Just checking on you, Aunt Ruby. You have someone to put your shutters up?" Ruby wasn't technically her aunt, but she and her siblings had grown up calling both Ruby and Judith "aunt."

"Of course." Ruby gave her a last squeeze and then slipped behind a small, glass counter. She picked up her cell phone, checked it. "The house is taken care of. I'm actually staying at a friend's."

Mila caught the mischievous sparkle in her eye and smiled. Ruby had never married, preferring to live as a free spirit when it came to relationships. "Good for you."

They glanced up at the sound of footsteps on the stairs. Two guests of the B&B were making their way downstairs from one of the five guest rooms. They were in their seventies and well-dressed. The man clutched a suitcase, and the woman had a black carry-on bag.

Ruby helped them check out and listened as they raved about their stay, their accents British or Australian... Mila could never tell. That probably meant she needed to take her mother up on her offer of traveling with her. Maybe one day. She busied herself looking at the containers of crystals, handmade jewelry and metaphysical books for sale.

"See you next year," Ruby called as they waved once more at the door.

Mila returned to the counter. "How many guests do you have staying here?"

"They were the last. I don't want the liability of guests during a hurricane." Her thin lips, stained with berry-colored lipstick, suddenly twisted with worry. "I tried to call Judith, but she didn't pick up."

Mila shifted on her feet. "Yeah. I'm heading over there next."

Her head cocked like she was listening to something and then she nodded. "Your Grandma is very proud of the woman you've become."

Mila unexpectedly felt a knot in her throat. Ruby was the only one who referred to her grandma in the present tense, like she was still around. Who knows. Maybe she is. Mila cleared her throat. "Well, I better head over to Judith's."

Ruby shook her finger, sending silver bracelets clinking down her bony forearm. "She puts on a good face, but don't let her fool you. She's named that gator in her lake Fred like it's some gosh-darn pet. Talks to it, too."

Mila felt a pang of guilt at that news. She should have checked on her sooner. "Thanks for the head's up."

※

Ruby and Judith couldn't be more different, but they had the same heart, the same compassion for Edgewater and its people. An important foundation for friendship.

Judith had retired from Edgewater City Council and had also been the mayor's council chair, where she'd served for over twenty years. Despite her short 5'4" stature, she'd been a fierce advocate for keeping Edgewater a small village community, successfully capping the building heights to three stories and battling to keep big box stores out of their town limits so the local businesses could flourish. She also made a killer key lime pie, Mila's favorite dessert.

Mila drove east through downtown and into Golfwood Estates, an established neighborhood of about eighty brick, ranch-style houses built around a teardrop-shaped lake with a golf course behind it. The lawns were perfect green squares and the roads were dappled with shadows from the mature oak trees. A few of the neighbors were outside doing hurricane prep, bringing in plants, yard ornaments and anything else that could become projectiles. They gave friendly waves to her as she passed.

Judith's white BMW was parked in the driveway in front of her red brick home. Mila slid her SUV into the space beside it, walked down her beautifully landscaped path to the front door and knocked.

A dog barked and after a few seconds, Judith opened the door. "Mila! What a nice surprise, dear. Come in, come in." Judith was wearing a red apron, waving a wooden spoon around. Her short, ash-gray hair was a ball of frizz, and her smile pushed into her plump cheeks. Gordon Ramsay, her overweight terrier-mix with one eye, waddled behind her, tail wagging. They'd named him after the volatile TV Chef after he'd turned up his nose at commercial dog food as a pup.

"Didn't catch you at a bad time, I hope." Mila reached down and scratched Ramsay under the chin. Then she followed Judith through an open living room into the kitchen, where butter and garlic smells were wafting from the stove. "Smells delicious."

"Thank you and don't be silly. It's never a bad time for a visit. Sit." She moved some Home Decor magazines off a bar stool and gave Mila's arm a squeeze. Her hand was warm and soft. "Tell me what brings you. Everything good? Harper okay?"

Mila noticed Judith's late husband John's cigar box was still out on the counter. John had passed from cancer seven months ago. "She's fine. I was actually just checking to make sure you had someone to help you put your hurricane shutters up."

"Oh." Judith moved around to the other side of the counter and stirred whatever was in the pot on the stove. "You think that's necessary?"

"I think it's a good precaution, yes."

Judith reached into the knife holder and plucked out a pair of meat scissors. She moved a large plate of raw chicken to the sink, so she could talk to Mila as she cut. "Those weather people, they get everyone in a panic for nothing. Just a little rain and wind."

Mila eyed the large pieces Judith was cutting. A lot bigger than the ones already cooked and on a plate by the stove. She glanced over at the couch where Ramsay had settled on a pillow with his snout between his paws. He knew the chicken wasn't for him. Mila glanced out the bay window, where the lake's blue waters sparkled about a dozen feet from her pool cage. A familiar shape floated just off the shoreline.

By the size of the gator's head, it was about six or seven feet. Large enough to pull a five-foot-four woman into the water.

"Aunt Judith, are you cutting up that chicken for the gator?"

She frowned. "Well, if I don't, he'll just swallow it whole."

Mila stared at her. *Was she showing signs of dementia?* "Aunt Judith." Mila waited until she met her eyes. "You know making that gator comfortable around humans will be signing his death warrant. This isn't like you, what's going on?"

Judith's shoulders fell and tears magnified her pale gray eyes. She pushed her glasses up and wiped beneath them with a potholder. "You're right. I don't know what's wrong with me. It's just... I don't know what to do with myself. John and I, we did everything together and now that he's gone, I just feel so alone." Her voice cracked.

Mila walked around the counter and folded her into a tight hug. Ruby was right. Judith wasn't handling John's death as well as everyone thought. "You're not alone, though. You have Ruby, me, Harper and Kittie. You know Kittie would be glad to have the company while Harper's in school. Call her anytime."

"I will." Judith pulled away and patted Mila's hand, still sniffling. "I'll call her."

Mila glanced out the window and smirked. "And maybe get another dog?"

Judith's chuckle turned into a long sigh. "I miss your grandma, too. We had some good times." She waved a hand. "Anyway, how's your mother? I haven't heard from her in a month."

Mila leaned against the counter. "She's at a retreat in the mountains, should be back next week." Mila checked the time on her Fitbit. She needed to head out. "I have to go, but back to my original question."

Judith stuck a hand on her ample hip. "Lordy, you've always been a stubborn one. All right, I'll call Marcus, my lawn guy. He'll put 'em up for me." She walked Mila to the door. "Heard about that young mother who died. Such a shame. The news alert said it was a possible suicide?"

Mila sighed. "It wasn't. But let's keep that between us while we investigate."

"Oh. This world." Judith reached out and wrapped thick arms around her. "Be careful out there. That daughter of yours needs her mother."

By the time Mila got back to the station, it was almost six. A few news vans were parked in the lot and Mila recognized Elly Prescott in the small group of reporters gathered outside the doors. Mila held up a hand to stop their questions as she passed through their gathering. "Don't you all have a hurricane to report on?" She slipped quickly into the building.

Frank and Aiden were back in the bullpen at their desks.

"The vultures are circling out there." She sighed as she fell into her chair and dropped her bag on the floor.

Aiden spun his chair around and smirked at her. "Yeah, someone at the crime scene fell to Elly Prescott's charm. Her breaking news article this morning had way too much detail, and of course a video of Ms. Anderson's bagged body being loaded into the ME van. Then another breaking news alert two hours later with the vic's name. Have you seen it?"

Mila groaned and reached for the water bottle she'd abandoned on her desk this morning. "Nope but I've run into plenty of people today who have." She took a long pull from the bottle and then ask, "What did you and Frank get?"

"Joey Bingham is the boyfriend." Yeah, Mila had learned that from Cara's sister, but she didn't interrupt him. "The couple who live across the hall confirmed there were many loud arguments from their apartment before Cara had Rose. They also saw her with a black eye and bloody lip more than once. The woman," he checked his notes, "Trish Jones, who lives in the apartment right next door actually gave Cara the name of a shelter to go to. This was back before Cara had Rose, also."

"Did Cara go? To the shelter?" Mila asked.

"Miss Jones didn't know. But a few weeks after Cara had Rose, she didn't see Bingham around anymore. The Domestic Violence program and shelter is run by Christ Fellowship Church, they want a warrant to reveal if Cara came to them for help, so Frank's working on that."

Mila crossed her ankle over her knee and leaned back, thinking. "Maybe Cara got the courage to kick Bingham to the curb when she had Rose. Maybe protecting the baby became her priority." That certainly made sense to Mila. "I got a new address for Bingham from the last arresting officer. Guess we should head back to Tampa and see if he's home. You got anything else to follow up on?"

Aiden stood and stretched. "Not until that warrant for the Domestic Violence Program at the church comes through." He grabbed his sports jacket off the back of his chair. "Get some dinner on the way?"

"Actually, I need to check on Harper. There was an incident at school today. We can grab some food from the house. You know Kittie always has vegetarian options. Just give me one sec." She pulled out her notebook and headed for Matt's office.

"Hey, Matt." Mila stood in the doorway of his office, which was extraordinarily organized. She held up a mug of coffee, black with two sugars like he liked it. "I have coffee."

He waved her in. "I would never turn down caffeine, thanks." Matt's thick, black hair was standing up in front like he'd stuck his hand through it in frustration too many times, the sleeves on his white dress shirt were rolled up, and he seemed distracted by whatever he was working on as his fingers clacked over the keyboard. Mila placed the coffee on a free coaster on his desk and gave him a second to finish.

"Okay. What else do you have for me?"

She gave him the names of Pastor Burns's family for a background check. "This is low priority. I need Cara's phone and computer info first."

"Well, luckily I didn't have to break into the phone. Her password was her daughter's name. A cursory check didn't show any texts or calls that night except to Fayth, the babysitter. Anything specific you're looking for when I take a deeper dive?"

"I need a summary of texts, calls, emails, photos she took of anyone in the past year. Messages from social media if they seem relevant. Anything deleted that may be relevant."

"Got it. Should have a report for you a few hours after the warrant comes in."

"You're the best."

Twelve

When Mila and Aiden walked through the front door, Harper was sitting across from Kittie at the table, both painting flowerpots. They would put plants in them and take them to retirement homes. It was one of their rituals when Harper was sad. Kittie believed that doing something kind for someone else was the cure for sadness, and they had all adopted her philosophy.

Oscar rose from his spot at Harper's feet to greet them. He scooped up his favorite pull toy and nudged Mila's hand to play. She reached down with both hands and gave him a good scratch on his chest. "Not now, boy." Tail wagging and still holding his toy hopefully, he moved on to Aiden, getting another scratch for the effort.

"Mom!" Harper slipped out of the chair and practically knocked Mila over with a hug. Then she peered around her mom. "Hi, Mr. Aiden."

"Hello, Harper. I see you've grown two feet since I saw you last."

Harper snorted and beamed at the same time. Mila closed her eyes, enjoying the brief moment her daughter was safe in her arms. Then Harper looked up, her puffy eyes full of indignation. "Guess what Mason did to Iggy today?"

Kittie caught Mila's eye as she rose from the table and winked. Mila feigned surprise. "Tell me."

They sat at the table, Harper gesturing wildly, as she told the story with all the flair for drama of a ten-year-old girl.

Iggy was in his aquarium on the vacant chair next to her, as if Harper couldn't bear to let him out of her sight. Mila understood this on a visceral level. When she'd had to go back to work and leave Harper for the first time, it was terrifying not being there, not being able to check on her breathing, her temperature, if she was hungry. She forced herself back to the present, where Harper was now at the climax of her story.

"He said Iggy should live out in the wild, but he had him zipped up in his backpack! Nothing to keep his temperature up. He could have killed him." Tears welled up in her eyes.

Mila reached over and took both of her daughter's hands in hers. "But he didn't. Iggy is safe and sound. That's what's important. What *did* happen, not what could've happened."

Harper nodded. A small smile pulled at the corner of her mouth as she said, "Hannah got in trouble for calling him an a-hole. Had to write him an apology letter." She pulled her hands away, picked up the paintbrush and continued swirling yellow paint to make a sun on the flowerpot.

Hannah was Harper's best friend and a real pistol. Mila had to hide her own smile. "She's a good friend. You're lucky to have her."

She peered over at Iggy, who was resting, his brown body flattened out on a basking rock, and asked quietly, "But do you think Iggy *should* be set free? Would he be happier?"

Kittie and Aiden were in the kitchen. They both stopped what they were doing and glanced at her. Even Oscar seemed to sense Harper's distress and rested his chin on her lap.

Mila stared at her daughter thoughtfully. "Bearded dragons aren't native to Florida. He would have a hard time surviving in the wild." Of course, Harper knew this already. She could rattle off a thousand facts about reptiles. But, she hoped it helped to hear it out loud. "What we could do is get him a larger home."

Harper tapped the tip of the paintbrush against her dimpled cheek, staring at Iggy as if she were consulting with him and then nodded. "Yeah. I think he would like that. Also, I think I should get him a harness and leash, so he can explore outside."

Aiden chimed in from the kitchen. "I've got a three-foot terrarium with a screen top in our garage you can have. Sidney went through a brief snake phase." He held up the bags with their packed dinners. A signal they were ready to head out.

"She had a pet snake?" Harper asked with a big grin.

"Don't even think about it." Mila laughed, kissed the top of her daughter's head, then nodded at Aiden in both acknowledgment and gratitude.

Traffic was heavy, people heading home from work compounded with people still out trying to gather hurricane supplies. They were crossing Old Tampa Bay's dark blue waters, which now churned with whitecaps—via Courtney Campbell Causeway—when Aiden took a video call from his three young daughters. They were all talking at once and somehow he held a conversation with all of them. Mila smiled and shook her head as the chaos was interrupted by his wife's voice when she took over the phone. She tuned out to give them some privacy. There was enough drama in her life with one daughter, she couldn't imagine three.

As she continued on State Road 60, she felt her body reacting to being so close to the University of Tampa and the off-campus rental house she'd called home for two years. The house her friend, Sabine, had died in. Her stomach clenched and her breathing grew shallow. She tried to conjure up the good memories.

Mila had been awarded a full scholarship that allowed her to pursue a psychology degree and swim for the Spartans.

Her first year she'd set a record for the 100 Individual Medley and got to swim in the Division 11 National Championships. She was living her dream. But after that fateful night, Mila couldn't go back to school. To say her father was disappointed was an understatement. Of all people, as a cop, he should've understood when you witness violence like that, it changes you. You spend thousands of moments imagining just one thing different, one thing that would've altered the outcome. Maybe there are multiverses… and in one of them, Sabine had survived and was living her dream of being a journalist.

After an hour on the road, Mila was happy to get out of the SUV and stretch when they pulled into Blue Cove Apartment Complex. Glancing up at the sky, she took note of the white and gray cirrus clouds rolling in from the outer bands of Henry. Evidence of the impending storm was in the air, too, in the form of a pressure drop and a cooler tropical breeze. She adjusted her belt and slipped into her blazer. Aiden did the same, then they headed toward the square, rundown brick building. The elevator was broken, so they trudged up six flights of stairs to find 632 B. The narrow hallway was dim and smelled like mildew and fried food.

Aiden stood to the side while Mila pounded on the door. "Joey Bingham, Edgewater PD. Open up. We need a word." She repeated this several times, louder each time before the door flew open and a skinny, shirtless man covered in tattoos stood there glaring at them.

"Yo, what the fuck is your problem? I have neighbors you know."

Mila smirked and shoved the door open, catching him off-guard and sending him stumbling back a few feet. The place reeked of weed. "We just need a few minutes of your time, Mr. Bingham."

Aiden stepped in behind Joey and then moved closer to his side as he whirled around to glare at Mila. The man's beady gaze darted around like he wasn't sure if he had anything to hide. "You can't just come in here without a warrant."

Mila was already peering into the bedroom to make sure they were alone, though anyone could've been hiding under the piles of clothes strewn over the brown carpet. She casually stepped back around the sofa and held out her hands. "Like I said, we just want to talk."

He folded his arms across his bare chest. "About what?"

"Cara Anderson."

His eyes narrowed and his face turned blood red. "That ho?" He scoffed. "I ain't seen her in months so I have no idea about her life right now." He waved a hand like he was swatting a fly. "Good fuckin' riddance."

Mila took a few steps closer but made sure she angled her hip with her Glock away from the agitated man. "Interesting choice of words."

Joey squirmed under her scrutiny, but his mouth clamped shut.

She took another step forward, so she was only a few feet from him. "Tell me more about how you are happy to get rid of Cara. Because someone murdered her last night."

Mila watched the confusion and then the reality of what she'd just said play out on his face. The color drained away beneath his stringy facial hair, and he walked stiffly to the sofa and let his body fall like a small tree that had just been chopped down.

They gave him a moment to process the news, both watching carefully as he sniffed and wiped at his nose with the back of his hand. When he finally cleared his throat and returned their gaze Aiden asked, "Where were you last night between nine and one a.m., Joey?"

He was staring at Aiden, but his mind was still lost in the news of Cara's death. Aiden repeated the question and Joey finally pushed out some hoarse words that gave away his emotions. "I was with Heather. We played some pool at Angie's Bar, had some beers, and got back here around one in the morning."

"I'm going to need a full name and phone number for Heather."

"Heather Browne." He rattled off her number.

Aiden jotted that down and glanced up at Mila. If his alibi checked out, he wasn't their guy. They wouldn't waste much more time here. "Tell me about the last time you saw Cara."

Joey swiped an arm across his nose and sniffed. "It was the day I moved out of our place." He pushed a hand through his hair and grew agitated. "Rose was four weeks old. She woke up one night just cryin' like the devil, nothing Cara did was makin' her stop. I had to work early the next morning so... well, we got into a fight and Cara blurted out that her and Rose didn't need me. That Rose wasn't even mine anyway."

The following ticks of silence were filled with an electric charge. "That must've really made you angry." Mila kept her tone non-judgmental.

His eyes blazed, his hands balled into fists. "It made me feel like an idiot. We'd always used protection, so I should've known it wasn't mine. I asked her who she'd... slept with but she wouldn't tell me."

Mila imagined how that conversation must have gone, in the middle of the night with tensions high from a crying baby. Maybe the only thing that saved Cara from a beating was the baby she was holding. "What did you do then?"

He held his hands out like it was obvious. "I packed my shit and left. No use supportin' a kid that's not even mine."

"Of course." Mila bit her tongue. "And you haven't seen Cara since that night?"

"Hell no. Why would I?"

Maybe to make sure she was okay after years of being used as a punching bag, you selfish jackass. "What did Cara do for work?"

"She'd been working some shifts at the SpookEasy Lounge in Ybor. She had to quit after Rose was born. Paying someone to watch Rose would've been more than she could make. She got real serious about her art then. Had shells and glass and shit all over the house. Started selling it online, but I don't know how she paid rent after I left, honestly. Maybe she got a roommate." His fingers made imaginary quotes around "roommate" as his face darkened.

The poor girl was dead, and he was still pissed at her for betraying him. Mila glanced at Aiden. He nodded. They were done here. "All right, thanks for your time, Mr. Bingham."

When they got back in the SUV, Aiden called Heather Browne. She confirmed she was with Joey all night. "We need to swing by Angie's Bar and make sure she's not lying to cover for him."

"Yeah." Mila took a swig from her water bottle, then said, "We also need to find out who Rose's father is. She didn't even tell her sister, Charlie, who he is. Why the big secret?"

Mila's phone dinged with a text. It was from Charlie. She scanned it and then said, "Speaking of, Charlie is back at Cara's house with Rose. Child Services gave them a ride over. She's going to pack up her sister's stuff tomorrow."

Aiden was rummaging through their dinner bag and pulled out a granola bar. "That's good news." He paused opening the bar and his eyes flashed. "Did you notice Bingham didn't even ask what was going to happen to Rose. What an asshole. Also, if I have the timeline right, Cara moved to Edgewater just four weeks after he moved out. How did she have the money to move and pay first and last month's rent in Edgewater if she wasn't working?"

Mila tapped her fingers on the steering wheel. "The landlord said she was a good tenant, never late with rent. Those houses are worth half a million now, so I'm sure the rent was high." Mila remembered Fayth telling her about Cara's online store. "Let me check something." She pulled up Etsy on her phone and typed in "Salty Sea Art," then clicked open the shop. There were six pieces of Cara's beach art listed for sale. "There are only a few reviews on Cara's Etsy shop so I'm guessing she hadn't made very many sales. You're right, the math isn't adding up. Hopefully Matt will have her financials soon. Then we'll see." She punched SpookEasy Lounge in the GPS. "Before we swing by Angie's Bar, let's go talk to her former place of employment."

The décor of the Spookeasy Lounge matched Mila's mood with its black brick walls, oversized black leather and red velvet chairs, heavy red curtains and decorations of skeletons, skulls, candelabra chandeliers and other goth items. Including an animated, spooky hologram painting Mila locked eyes with as they walked through the room to the bar. This place got an A for atmosphere. She was temporarily distracted by the three arched gothic windows behind the bar with artificial blue flames rippling through them. In the middle of the back wall was what looked like a large reaper in a cloak, flanked by two gargoyles. She shared an amused eyebrow raise with Aiden.

"Welcome, what can I get for you?" The bartender asked after she set down two glass skulls in front of the couple beside them.

Mila held up her badge. "The manager, please."

The woman's smile faded. "Oh, okay." She glanced around. "Let me go grab her."

Mila busied herself reading the non-alcoholic drink menu as they waited. "Can I interest you in a Zombie Cold

Brew? Or maybe a Ghostly Growler?" Mila grinned at Aiden. He was reading a menu, too.

"Actually I think it would be a shame to come here without trying the Blood Orange Ginger Kombucha. You should try something... get out of your comfort zone."

"I like my comfort zone, it's... comforting."

A thirty-something woman in a black pantsuit and dark ponytail approached them and held out her hand. "Hi, I'm Gretchen, the manager. How can I help you?"

Mila shook her hand. "Detective Harlow, Edgewater PD. This is Detective Reyes." She waited until Gretchen shook Aiden's hand and then continued. "We're here about Cara Anderson. We were told she worked here?"

"Oh, Cara, yes. But she hasn't worked here for six months or so." She crossed her arms and let her gaze flick between the two detectives. "Is she okay?"

Mila held her gaze. "No, actually. She was murdered two days ago."

Gretchen's hands rose and covered her mouth and nose as she shook her head. She lowered herself onto a barstool, her face pale with shock. "Oh my God, she'd just had a baby."

"Did she ever mention who the baby's father was?"

"No. We weren't that close to discuss things like that, but I know she was living with her boyfriend." Her eyes widened. "Did he kill her?" A tiny nose piercing winked as her nostrils flared. "She came to work more than once with a bruise on her face. I should've done something."

Mila rested a hand on her arm briefly to pull the woman out of the spiral of guilt she was falling into. "We don't think it was her boyfriend." When Gretchen finally nodded, Mila asked, "Is there anything else you can think of that may help? Maybe a customer that had a problem with Cara? Another employee?"

Gretchen was shaking her head when the bartender leaned on the counter, her small chin, shaved head and large eyes gave her an alien-like appearance. "Excuse me, I didn't mean to eavesdrop, but Cara did tell me she felt like she had a stalker."

Mila and Aiden shared a glance. Then she asked, "Did she mention a name?"

A small shrug. "No, she didn't know who it was. Just noticed the same white car with front-end damage following her to work, enough times to get creeped out. The person was wearing sunglasses and a hoodie, which seemed more suspicious to her."

"But they never approached her? Threatened her?"

"No. As far as I know just followed her."

Mila slid her card to the bartender. "If you can think of anything else, please give me a call." She nodded to Gretchen. "Thanks for your time."

"What do you think about the stalker theory?" Aiden asked as they pulled away from the bar into heavy traffic. "Maybe Rose's bio dad?"

"Maybe. If only we knew who he is." Mila signaled and switched lanes, squeezing behind a line of cars at the red light to make a left.

"Or the ex's new girlfriend, Heather Browne? Maybe she wanted to make sure they were really broken up."

"That would be easy to check." Mila typed Heather Browne's name into the DMV database. "No. The car registered to her is a 2016 GMC truck. Black." Then she typed Angie's Bar into the GPS. "But let's confirm her and the ex's alibi so we don't waste any more time on them."

Mila found herself scanning every white car for front-end damage as they drove. She turned up the radio when she heard the weather report. "Henry's winds are now at 95 mph, right on the cusp of becoming a Category 2 storm. A tornado watch is still in effect for the west coast as Henry's path continues as expected. The Hurricane Center computer data now puts landfall somewhere between Clearwater and

Tarpon Springs. Evacuation orders have been issued for all residents in low-lying areas and mobile homes in the following counties..." Mila sighed and turned down the radio after hearing their county listed. Edgewater was still in the running for landfall.

After the owner of Angie's Bar—who was actually a man in his seventies named Bruno—kindly showed them video of Joey and Heather leaving a little before one in the morning, they crossed the two off their suspect list.

Mila's phone pinged with a notification. She steered the SUV into a parking lot and pulled up the email. It was a preliminary report from the ME including a tox screen. "Looks like no fingerprints on the knife or wine bottle. Not even Cara's."

"Wiped then," Aiden said, the frustration evident in his tone.

"Yep. But there were traces of benzos in the wine bottle, and..." She scanned the email: *Specimens tested from cardiac blood, urine, vitreous eye fluid laid out in tabular form with the measured concentrations of substances found in each.* "And seems the tox screen found high doses of benzos in the vic's system along with the alcohol. Interesting. Her blood alcohol level was .16. Pretty high." Mila looked up from her phone. "She would've had to almost drink the whole bottle of wine herself. As far as the Benzos, though... she did have benzos in her medicine cabinet, but the perscription was almost full, so I don't think those were hers." Aiden grew thoughtful. Mila read on. "The hair was medium coarseness, wavy, black, with no signs of chemical processing. Hair with root ball sent for nuclear DNA testing."

"Well, that's something to go on," Aiden said.

Another alert pinged. Mila glanced down at her phone. "And that would be the report from Matt on our vic's phone and computer. Looks like a large file." She tossed her phone in the console. "I think we're done in Tampa for now. Let's go back to the station where we can read this on the computer."

Aiden was checking his phone. "Hold that thought." He held it up. "Frank just forwarded the warrant for Christ Fellowship Church."

Mila checked the time. Almost nine. She punched in the address in the GPS. "Let's go see if anyone's there."

The church was a fairly modern-looking rectangular building with brick and stonework. There were a few cars in the parking lot under fluorescent lights, which was a good sign.

They stepped through the smoked glass double doors, into the cool, dimly lit interior. A chime announced their arrival.

A door opened to their left and a tall woman wearing a black midi dress, her gray hair in a tight bun and silver framed glasses stepped out to greet them. "Welcome." Her smile seemed to falter as she quickly assessed their business clothes and serious demeanor. To her credit, she crossed the room quickly and held out her hand. "Doris Burbury, Director. How can I help you?"

Mila introduced them and then presented her with the warrant they'd printed off in the SUV. "We need information on Cara Anderson. We were told she may have come here for help with a domestic violence situation."

Doris looked over the warrant, deep wrinkles appearing in her forehead. "Cara, yes." She glanced up sharply. "Is she okay?"

"I'm afraid she was murdered last night," Aiden said.

Doris squeezed her eyes shut and shook her head. "The boyfriend?"

"No, actually we've ruled him out. That's why we need your help," Mila said.

"Oh." Dark gray eyes widened in surprise. "Of course. Follow me." She led them into her office, and they took a seat in front of her desk as she rummaged through a file cabinet against the back wall and plucked out a folder. "Here it is." She handed the folder to Aiden. "That's her information she filled out. I'll pull up my notes." Her roller chair squeaked as she sat down and wiggled the mouse on her desk. The monitor light reflected blue in her glasses as she typed.

"The date is 1 year and 4 months ago," Aiden read. "Says Joey left bruises on her neck and she was afraid for her life, also too afraid to go to the police. That would just make him madder." He lifted a Polaroid from the file and showed it to Mila. It was a close-up of Cara's face and neck, eyes haunted and swollen, black bruises in the shape of fingers on her pale throat.

Mila's chest tightened as fury and sadness rose up from wherever they resided within her when she had them under control. If only they could go back in time with the knowledge they had now and save her. She looked at Aiden. "So, she came here for help a month before she got pregnant with Rose. She never went to the police."

Doris glanced up sharply. "She had a baby? What will happen to her?"

"Cara's sister has agreed to be her guardian," Mila answered.

"That's at least some good news." A printer whirled to life on a table behind Doris. She got up to retrieve the paper. "Unfortunately, I don't have much for you. Cara only came to one appointment after our initial meeting, so we never got to create a full plan to help her leave her situation." She handed the printed paper to Mila and took a seat back behind her desk. "I wondered what happened to her. Such a shame."

Mila read the Director's notes. Nothing stood out. "Did she ever mention feeling like someone else was following her?"

Doris's brows pinched together. "No. Not to me anyway."

Mila handed the notes to Aiden. "Tell me more about what you do here. Who's involved in the process?"

Doris adjusted her glasses and leaned against her desk. "When a woman first comes in our priority is to get her medical attention if she needs it. Then we feed her and offer her a safe place to spend the night. We have one volunteer counselor on site twenty-four hours and a large community of volunteers that do things like help identify the woman's needs, gather the resources, clothing, transportation, and placement in one of our shelters, depending on whether they have children or pets. Help them secure employment if they don't have an income." She sighed. "But like I said, we didn't have a chance to do that with Cara. She didn't want to stay the night. She was afraid her boyfriend would think she was with another guy, and he would kill her. She came once after that and then just disappeared."

"Can I get the names of everyone she was in contact with here?" Mila stood and put her card on the desk. "Be great if you could email me that list tonight."

"Anything I can do to help." Doris stood and shook their hands with a firm grip. "I hope you find who did this to her. She didn't deserve it."

Thirteen

When they returned to the station, Francine had left for the day, and it was quiet. Mila's eyes were dry and burning as she dropped into her chair and pulled up the file Matt had sent her. She took a swig of the gas station coffee they'd stopped for as Aiden pulled his chair around and they went through it together, starting with Cara's phone data. The night before the murder there was a call from Gulf Shores Community Church that lasted four minutes.

Aiden's chair squeaked as he leaned back and laced his hands behind his head. "Maybe the pastor's wife checking on her? Maybe she lied about Cara's state of mind? What would be the motive for her to lie, though?"

Mila sighed. "No idea."

After a few more minutes, Mila leaned forward and tapped the monitor. "Here. She received a text two hours before she left the house last night, and deleted the number. Matt has a note here: *This is a burner number I traced back to an app called HydeMe. You can get the IP address of the user from them and then I can get their Internet Service Provider to give us the contact info of that IP address.*" Her tiredness waned a bit with the excitement of this new information. She glanced over at Aiden.

He nodded, a new light in his tired eyes, also. "You keep reading. I'll work on the warrant for HydeMe."

Mila didn't see anything else of concern in Cara's phone records, so she moved to the laptop information.

Captain Bartol appeared from her office, her bag over her shoulder, the slight limp in her walk she got when she'd been sitting too long and her knee acted up. "I saw the preliminary lab report, no fingerprints but traces of Benzos in the wine bottle. Looks like that's what was used to incapacitate her. What else have we got?"

Mila filled her in on everything they'd learned in the last few hours, from ruling out the ex-boyfriend to the burner number that had texted her hours before her death, and Cara having a possible stalker. "I'm about to dig into her laptop data now."

Captain Bartol adjusted her bag, shifted her weight. "The stalker could be Rose's biological father. The shoe print beneath the window would make sense then. Maybe Cara wouldn't give him access to his daughter, and so he killed Cara and was going to take Rose. Let's face it, she didn't have a great track record in choosing the men in her life."

"True." Mila rubbed her stiff shoulder. "But according to Fayth, the bio dad didn't want anything to do with Rose. That could've been a lie, I suppose. And Fayth did say she fell asleep on the couch with Rose, so Rose wasn't in her room that night. Maybe he abandoned that plan after seeing the empty crib."

Captain Bartol nodded. "Then it's possible Rose is still in danger. Where's the kid now?"

A rush of adrenaline shot through Mila at the thought of Rose being in danger. "She's with Cara's sister, Charlie, at the house. She's going to pack up Cara's things tomorrow. You think we should post a uniform there to keep an eye on her?"

The captain's expression reflected Mila's concern. "I'll call Sergeant White. By the way, I sent Frank home for a few hours of sleep, he didn't look too hot, but if you need him for anything, wake him up. If you don't find anything to track down tonight, catch a few hours yourselves. We'll regroup at

6 a.m. I have a feeling Henry's going to interrupt this investigation."

"Yes Ma'am." Mila's brows pressed down. *Was Frank sick?* She shook off the thought, she didn't have time to worry about that right now. She scrolled to the part of Matt's report that had Cara's laptop information. She carefully read each line of the bank statements. "Interesting."

Aiden swiveled around and stared at her hopefully. "What have you got?"

Mila glanced up at him over her monitor. "A four-thousand-dollar cash deposit three weeks before Cara moved to Edgewater. And..." she scrolled, "a three-thousand-dollar cash deposit two months after she moved here."

"So, explains how she could afford to move. But cash... not traceable. And from who?"

Mila picked up her phone and texted Charlie: *did u give Cara 4,000 cash or 3,000 cash?*

Charlie texted back right away: *No. She never asked for money.*

Mila dropped her phone on the desk. "Not from the sister. Let me check her emails and socials, see if there was a secret sugar daddy."

Her emails were mostly spam and her social media was pretty bare, just photos of Rose, mostly. They were hard to look at. The baby was so happy and Cara seemed happy. Of course, social media could be deceiving, but it sure looked like Rose had changed her life, and had given her a reason to smile.

Another half hour went by. Mila was just about to get up and see if there was coffee left in the breakroom, when an email came in. It was the list of people from Christ Fellowship Church. "Aiden, I'm forwarding you the list from Doris Burbury. Can you go through the people Cara would've come in contact with and see if you can find a connection to Edgewater or Cara outside of the program?"

Aiden lifted his coffee cup into the air without turning around. His determination was still intact as he replied, "On it."

Mila stood, put in some eyedrops and stretched her back, then clicked back to the file with Cara's computer information while standing. She forced herself to slow down and read each line instead of scrolling. It paid off. She found a line that she'd missed. "Well, this looks promising." She glanced up. Aiden was staring at her expectantly, so she continued. "There's a file called *private journal*. It's password protected. There's an asterisk here with a note that Matt needs some more time to crack it."

Aiden's cheeks puffed out then he blew out a long breath, hands clasped behind his head. "It'd be great if she named Rose's father and who gave her that money. *If* Matt can get in it. We may have to send it off to the digital forensics guys."

"That would take way too long. You know how backed up they are." Mila stared at the words *private journal*, wondering what kind of secrets were trapped in there, waiting to be uncovered. Hopefully ones that will help them find Cara's killer. "I have faith in Matt."

※

"Okay, I'm done." Another hour had crawled by with nothing to show for it. Mila leaned back and rubbed her stiff neck with a growl of frustration. "I don't think there's anything else to find here. No secret emails or messages on her socials from anyone she had a relationship with, no mention of money, no mention of Rose." She rested her chin on her fist, feeling every muscle in her body ache for a stretch. "We're missing something, though. She had to be communicating with whoever gave her that cash."

Aiden swiveled his chair around to face her and ran his hands roughly over his face. They sat in silence for a few seconds, the only sound was the hum and click of the air conditioner. Finally, Aiden spoke. "Maybe she had a burner phone or used the HydeMe app, too?"

Mila shook her head. "Matt would've found the app on her phone, even if she'd deleted it. I guess I could've missed a burner in Cara's house. Or Cara could've taken it with her the night she was killed, and the killer took it with them."

Aiden pointed a finger at her. "That actually makes sense. The killer wouldn't want the phone found, if that's how they were communicating with Cara."

Mila grabbed her coffee mug and glanced in at the dregs at the bottom, changed her mind and sat it back on the desk. "True. I just don't get it, though. Why use a burner phone? Why all the secrecy?"

"My guess... it's about the father of that baby or the money. Maybe she was blackmailing someone? Maybe they got tired of paying her."

"Maybe it's about both." Mila rubbed the back of her stiff neck. "You find connections with someone from Christ Fellowship Church?"

He shook his head, frustration carving lines in his forehead. "There are sixteen names, mostly women, no connection to Edgewater. The four men are older, one's the pastor of the church. I even ran each one to see if they owned a white Toyota. I can't see any of them being involved."

Mila checked her FitBit. It was almost midnight. "Let's call it a night. Meet you back here at 6 a.m. I'm going to just drive by Cara's house and make sure there's a patrol car there before I go home." The fact that Rose may be in danger meant so was Charlie.

※

When Mila pulled into her driveway thirty minutes later, satisfied that Charlie and Rose were safe, her headlights swept over the sandbags piled up against the garage door. She texted a "thanks to u & the boys" to Paul and then added.

"Think Kittie & Harper should come to ur place tomorrow. They've canceled schools." She waited a second and got the ping with a thumb's up emoji. He was up late as usual. She stopped herself from wondering what he was doing. *None of your business anymore.*

Mila opened Harper's bedroom door, letting her eyes adjust to the soft glow of her daughter's unicorn nightlight. A thumping came from Oscar's dog bed next to Harper's as he wagged his tail. Quietly, she made her way to the canopy bed, careful to avoid the floorboard that squeaked beneath the plush, cream carpeting, and stared down at her daughter. Her face was so peaceful, mouth slightly open with a light snore. A book on reptiles and a reading light lay on top of her chest. Mila moved them to her daughter's nightstand, kissed her warm cheek and whispered, "I love you to the moon and back." Then she gave Oscar a belly scratch and clicked the door closed softly behind her.

She changed into the worn-thin, gray Bradenton Police Academy T-shirt she'd hidden from Paul when he'd moved out. It didn't smell like him anymore, but it was a small comfort, a tiny reminder of him that made her feel safe. As she slid beneath the cool sheets, her muscles tense and achy, her mind began to tangle up images of Cara's body with Sabine's and her sister Harper's, until she fell into a restless sleep. When her alarm beeped at 5 a.m. she woke groggy and unsettled from the nightmares.

She took a hot shower, using a loofah and handfuls of creamy soap to scrub her skin raw, trying to wake up her body and wash away the images from her dreams. Then she blow-dried her hair, put on some tinted sunscreen, concealer for her dark under-eye circles and some blush to make sure she didn't look like a corpse herself. Her eye caught on the thick scar running down her neck in the mirror. Funny, she didn't even notice it much anymore. Once she'd got her shield, she'd stopped being angry every time she looked at it.

Instead, it became a symbol of being a survivor, not a victim. A symbol of strength. Of course, out in public, she might as well be wearing a sign that said, "I went through something horrific and am damaged goods." The questions and sympathy always surfaced in strangers' eyes.

Next she slipped into a fresh pair of black slacks, light blue Edgewater PD polo shirt and her duty belt. She opened the biometric safe in her closet and retrieved her Glock.

Kittie and Harper could sleep in since the county had canceled school for the next few days. If they missed too many, hurricane days would be made up in the summer. She shouldered her bag and slipped silently out the front door. The world that greeted her had changed.

A thick, gray cloud shelf now dominated the still-dark sky, and a light drizzle of rain was being blown in different directions. The gulf waters were choppy and loud, crashing into the seawall, sending foam tumbling across the two-lane road. A sudden gust of wind, at least twenty miles an hour, lifted the hair from her shoulders and a shiver wracked her body as she felt the promise of the damaging winds to come. She'd checked her phone while quickly eating a piece of peanut butter toast. Henry was experiencing rapid intensification and was a solid Cat 2. Also, landfall had been narrowed down to just south of Edgewater, which meant they would get the strong eyewall winds if that remained accurate. Not good news.

Windshield wipers going and headlights on, she stopped by Cara's house once again on her way to the station, chatting with the patrol officer for a minute. All was quiet last night. His replacement came while they talked under the small porch awning and Mila filled in Officer Gentry about the situation, making sure he knew they suspected Rose may be in danger. Before she climbed back into her SUV, she noticed the crows were gone. In fact, there was an eerie silence, an absence of wildlife chatter. The calm before the storm.

Fourteen

Frank was exiting his SUV in the station parking lot as she pulled up and shut off her engine. She grabbed her black, department-issued rain jacket with Edgewater PD on the back and flipped up the hood. No use walking around all day in damp clothes if she could help it. Frank waited for her, and they walked into the building together, but after the initial good morning exchange, he was silent, lost in his own thoughts. Mila didn't intrude. She had enough on her mind.

At 6:05 a.m. Captain Bartol and Matt were already in the conference room. The smell of buttery croissants and bitter coffee hung in the air. They exchanged good mornings and Mila took a seat beside Matt's wheelchair, greeting him with a nod, and pulled out her insulated coffee mug. She poured the dark, steaming liquid into it and then grabbed a still-warm croissant, hoping it would soak up the acid in her stomach.

Mila caught the captain's eye. "Tell Brigitte thanks for the croissants."

Captain Bartol offered her a distracted smile. "Will do."

Brigitte was Captain Bartol's wife of ten years, though they'd been together for almost twenty. Brigitte was also a former pastry chef and never let them have an early morning meeting without sending something delicious she'd baked. Hopefully, some caffeine and carbs would erase the brain fog Mila was feeling from stress and lack of sleep.

After Mila swallowed a bite, she turned to Matt, whose thick dark hair was still wet from either a shower or the rain.

"Great job on getting the deleted information from our vic's phone. Aiden got the warrant sent to HydeMe last night. Hopefully, they won't drag their feet."

He held up his coffee cup with the Edgewater PD logo. "Here's to a quick response."

Mila wanted to ask him about how long he thought opening Cara's private journal would take, but Aiden walked through the door with a cheerful, "Morning, all." His curls were still damp, and he also had on the department-issued rain jacket over his Edgewater PD polo. "I've got a number to harass them as soon as the sun comes up."

"Morning," Mila said as he took a seat across from her and reached for the coffee. There were purplish smudges beneath his eyes, too.

"All right. Let's go through what we have." Captain Bartol crumpled up her napkin, stood and grabbed a black whiteboard marker. She made a list of things they knew about Cara's life: Moved to Edgewater four months ago. She wrote "why?" next to that and underlined it twice.

Known Friends: Fayth Gandy, Stew Prescott and Alex Tremble."

"And Jemma Burns," Mila said after swallowing a warm mouthful of coffee.

"Right. She wasn't home when Frank tried to talk to her." After Captain Bartol added Jemma's name, she turned to Matt. "You finish the background checks on these people?"

He leaned forward in his wheelchair and tapped on a folder. "Fayth Gandy, Stew Prescott and Alex Tremble are clean. I haven't got to the pastor's family yet, though. I'll get that done this morning."

She put check marks by those three friends' names. "What else?" Captain Bartol held the marker over the board.

"The two cash deposits," Aiden said. "And her visits to Christ Fellowship Church in Tampa for domestic violence help. Though I didn't find any connection between the people our vic came in contact with at the church and Edgewater."

"The traces of Benzos in the wine bottle," Frank chimed in as the marker squeaked against the board. "Obviously why she didn't put up a fight."

"Also the dark, wavy hair found on her clothing," Mila added. "That should help when we get a suspect. We can do a comparison."

As the captain finished adding that, Mila swallowed her last bite of croissant and washed it down with a warm swig of coffee. "You know one thing I don't get, if this was a premeditated murder... which drugging the wine seems like it was, why did the killer use Cara's own knife to finish the job? Why didn't they bring their own weapon?"

Captain Bartol's gaze swept over the room, waiting to see if someone had a theory.

"Maybe it wasn't premeditated," Aiden offered. "Maybe they weren't planning on killing her, but just knocking her out for a while."

Frank wrapped his knuckles on the table. His face looked gaunt beneath a few days of stubble, his eyes puffy behind his glasses. "Don't forget about the shoeprint by the kid's window, and the neighbor possibly seeing someone lurking around midnight. Maybe they just wanted our vic out of the way for a few hours so they could take the kid?"

"So then the question is, who would want Rose?" Matt asked.

"Well, the father seems like the obvious suspect," Frank said. "Occam's razor."

Mila shifted in her chair. "We thought about that possibility, but I don't know. Cara told Fayth the father didn't want anything to do with the baby, remember? Yes, that could've been a lie, but why lie about that to her friend?"

"Unless the baby daddy lied to her," Frank said. "To keep her guard down."

Captain Bartol sighed as she stood at the board. "No use speculating about that point right now." She shifted the weight off her bad knee. "All right, what are we waiting on?"

"DNA from Rose's toothbrush and the hair with the root ball, and the information from HydeMe," Aiden offered.

Matt held up a pen he'd been using to take notes. "Also going to work on the vic's private journal file, hopefully get that cracked today. Maybe that will give us an answer about why she moved here."

"Good." Captain Bartol rubbed her forehead, thinking. "The DNA will probably take too long to help us identify the father, so hopefully she mentions him in the journal. Could we get so lucky?" A heavy sigh escaped her. "All right. I'm going to call a press conference before the weather deteriorates this morning and ask for the public's help. Frank, you feel up to checking with all the liquor stores in the area? It's a long shot, but maybe someone will remember who bought that bottle of Brea Chardonnay."

They all glanced at Frank. It didn't go unnoticed the way the captain had phrased her question.

Frank squirmed in his chair. "Of course."

Mila noticed he hadn't touched the coffee or croissants, instead nursing a water bottle. She shared an eyebrow raise with Aiden.

Captain Bartol continued. "Aiden, why don't you canvas Cara Anderson's neighborhood? If someone was sneaking around at midnight maybe there was a witness, or a ring camera that caught something." Then she turned to Matt. "You get on the rest of those background checks and cracking that journal." Her gaze found Mila. "What do you think your next step is?"

Mila had given a lot of thought to that very question. "I'm going to go talk to Jemma Burns. She's around Cara's age, so it's possible Cara would've felt more comfortable confiding in her about Rose's father or why she really came to Edgewater."

"All right. Let's hustle today, I don't have to remind you we're going to lose crucial investigation time to this damn hurricane. We've got until around dinner time before it's going to be too dangerous to be on the roads."

※

The sky was lightening up a bit as the sun rose, but all it did was highlight the fast-moving, charcoal clouds stretching south as far as the eye could see. Mila parked on Lime Street and slipped on her raincoat before heading toward the Burns's house where she hoped to find Jemma. But as she walked up the gravel drive, she noticed the door to the church was cracked open.

Approaching the door, she could hear deep sobbing echoing off the high ceiling, cutting through the silence of the empty room. The hair stood up on her arms. She recognized real pain when she heard it. Reflexively pushing her jacket out of the way and resting her hand on her Glock, she crept into the lobby, and pressed her back against the opened French door. Peering around the corner into the nave, she saw a figure kneeling at the altar rail. It was a girl. She was alone.

Relaxing, she removed her wet jacket, draped it across her arm and headed inside.

The girl was sobbing so hard, she didn't even realize Mila had walked in. Mila tossed her jacket on the first pew and moved up the two, carpeted steps to kneel beside the girl, who had her head hanging. Wavy, dark hair cut to her chin hid her face. Her hair and T-shirt were dry, so she must've been in here for a while.

"Hey," Mila said, touching her arm gently.

The girl startled, her sob cut short as she gasped. She stared wide-eyed at Mila, frozen. Her eyes were swollen, her nose red and dripping.

Mila held up her hands, showing she meant no harm. "I'm Detective Mila Harlow, Edgewater PD. Are you all right?"

The girl's shoulders slumped. She glanced away, pressed a wad of Kleenex against her nose. "Fine."

Mila smiled to herself. That was becoming Harper's favorite word, too. "That was the least convincing *fine* I've ever heard," she said softly. "And I have a ten-year-old daughter."

The girl's lip twitched, her watery eyes grazed Mila's face but then locked back on the flickering candles.

Mila tried again. "I actually came here to speak to Jemma. Would that be you?"

The girl squeezed her eyes shut, sending fresh tears rolling down her cheeks. "Yes."

"You heard what happened to Cara Anderson, I assume?"

A fresh sob escaped her. She wiped at her dripping nose without moving her gaze from the carpet. "Yes."

Mila didn't want to lead her to answers, but she had a feeling she'd be kneeling here all day if she waited until Jemma was ready to talk. "I understand that you and she were friends?"

Jemma shifted her body so she could face Mila. There was palpable fear in her wide, brown eyes. She pushed her hair behind her ears with shaking hands. "We were."

Mila kept her voice low so she didn't spook the girl. "Is that why you're so upset right now?"

Jemma nodded slowly, but her expression looked apprehensive, her body tense. She was in fight or flight.

Mila studied her. *Did she know something? Was she afraid Cara's attacker would come for her? This girl was* obviously traumatized, so she'd have to proceed delicately. "I know it's hard to lose a friend. Do you feel like you need to talk to someone? A grief counselor?"

Jemma pulled her feet up and wrapped her arms around her bare knees. She looked so young and vulnerable. "My mom is a counselor, so I can talk to her." Her attention shifted inward and she whispered, "I just don't know what to say."

"That's normal, Jemma." She waited until Jemma brought herself back from wherever her thoughts had taken her. She waited until she could hold her gaze. "Mr. and Mrs. Burns adopted you and your brother, correct?" Jemma nodded. "How old were you?"

A shiver went through her body, and she contracted herself into a tighter ball. "I was nine. My brother, Julian, was seven. I was in a foster home, and he was in a boys' home. They separated us. We didn't see each other for two years." Her expression softened and then fresh tears fell. "The Burns's saved our lives." She seemed to dissociate, and her tone flattened. "I would do anything for them."

Mila only nodded. She'd met enough people who suffered through one horror show foster home after another to know what Jemma must've gone through. At least she and her brother were finally together. She couldn't go down that rabbit hole right now though. "Jemma?" Again, she had to wait until the girl pulled herself out of her own thoughts. When she looked up, the fear was still there. "Can you tell me about the last time you saw Cara?"

At the mention of her friend's name, her head fell to her knees and her shoulders wracked with sudden, deep sobs again. Mila rested a hand on her back and waited for the wave of grief to pass. After a few minutes, Jemma lifted her head and blew her nose.

Her voice was a hoarse whisper. "I saw her Sunday at the late church service. We didn't really get a chance to talk though." Her attention caught on Mila's scar. "What happened to you?" Her eyes widened with panic. "Sorry, I didn't mean to be rude."

Mila held her gaze with a soft smile. "It's okay. I don't mind you asking. I actually was attacked in college. My roommate was killed, so it's kind of a reminder to me to be grateful I'm alive." She hoped one day Jemma could come to the same conclusion. That she would use the tragedy of losing her friend to appreciate every day.

"Oh. That's awful." She cocked her head curiously. "Did they catch the person? What happened to them?"

Mila nodded quickly. Jemma was probably looking for reassurance that her friend's killer would be caught. "Yes. He's in prison." She didn't mention they only got him on a second-degree murder charge because they couldn't convince the jury the murder was premeditated. The defense lawyer successfully argued it was a burglary gone wrong. The knife was taken from their kitchen on a whim. Twenty-four years. That's all he got. In a few years he'd be out in the world again. The same world that Harper lived in. Mila shook off the thought. That was a problem for another day.

Jemma eyed Mila and then seemed to come to a decision. "I have scars, too." She pulled her T-shirt off her shoulder and moved her hair out of the way. There were dozens of round scars over her shoulder and the back of her neck. "I ran away. Tried to find Julian. When I got caught and sent back, they used me as an ashtray."

Mila swallowed her horror and reached out, grabbed Jemma's hand in hers. It was ice cold. "I'm so sorry you went through that. You know you didn't deserve that, right? Those people that did that to you, they were monsters."

Jemma's chin fell. "I'd like to believe that. Sometimes I think I'm the monster." New tears fell as she slid her hand from Mila's and pulled her shirt back up. "I guess I should just be grateful to be alive, too. Like you said."

They sat in silence for a moment. Mila became aware of the time, knowing she was spending more of it here than she could afford. She brought the conversation back to the reason for her visit. "Jemma, did Cara ever confide in you who Rose's father was?"

Jemma's body stiffened at the mention of her friend's name. "No, we never talked about it."

Mila decided this would be the last question and she would leave the girl to grieve her friend in peace. "What about the reason she moved to Edgewater?"

Jemma's voice was a whisper again as she retreated back into her own mind. "She said she loved the town, the people."

Disappointment landed like a rock in her gut. "Okay, thank you." She pressed her card into Jemma's hand. "Please call me if you think of anything else Cara may have said that would help our investigation." She squeezed Jemma's forearm and got a small, sad smile from the girl. "Or just call if you need to talk. Anytime."

Mila stepped out of the church and a gust of wind lifted her jacket like bat wings. Needles of cold rain pricked her face. She paused to zip up her jacket. A young man came around the corner of the church with a wheelbarrow full of potted plants. It was the same person Pastor Burns had called "a good kid." *What was his name?* He paused when he saw her watching him.

She flipped up her hood and walked down to meet him in the yard. Lifting her jacket, she showed him her badge, then held out her hand. "Detective Harlow."

He removed a dirty work glove and shook it. His dark T-shirt was soaked and clinging to his body. "Santos. Santos Rosales."

That's right. Santos. "Nice to meet you. Pastor Burns speaks highly of you. Almost ready for the storm?"

Warm brown eyes lit up at the compliment. "Yeah, just taking in some last-minute things."

"Go ahead, I don't want to interrupt you." She walked by his side as he pushed the wheelbarrow up the driveway. "So, I was just talking to Jemma about Cara Anderson. How well did you know Cara?"

He paused to adjust his soggy baseball cap as another gust threatened to unseat it from his head. "Cara." He made the sign of the cross quickly over his chest. "Not good. She has not been in Edgewater for long. I see her in church, but we never really... you know... talked." He proceeded to push the wheelbarrow toward a standalone garage situated between the back of the church and the small house. He set it down in front of the doors. "She seemed like a nice girl. I'm sorry for what happened. I know she had a baby." He shook his head and glanced up at the sky, which was now just various shades of gray and black and spitting rain harder.

Mila caught her hood before the wind blew it off. She squinted against the rain pelting her face harder with every gust. "Who did you see her interact with at church?"

"Mostly Stew and Alex. You know them?" He glanced at Mila, and she confirmed with a nod. "And then only Jemma. She was good for my sister. Jemma, she is very..." he seemed to be struggling to find the word. Finally, he just tapped his head. "Inside here." Mila nodded her understanding.

The wooden garage door rattled as he squatted and lifted it up. An older model white Toyota Corolla sat in the shadows.

Mila scanned the car. No front-end damage. She reminded herself it was Florida. White was the preferred car color in a hot, sunny state. Still, she'd check the DMV, see if it was involved in any accidents. She walked around the back and snapped a photo of the license plate.

Santos carried the plants in and slid them against the wall. She couldn't think of anything else to ask him at the moment. "All right. I know you've got to get storm prep finished, so I'll let you get back to it. Stay safe." She gave him a card. "And please call if you think of anything that could help us."

He shoved the card in his shorts pocket, and then quickly glanced back at her. It was the kind of glance that made her suspicious he hadn't been honest with her.

Fifteen

Mila turned on the engine just in time to hear that Hurricane Henry's path had veered slightly north. Wind speeds hadn't changed. She drove by Judith's house to make sure she was ready. The lawn guy, Marcus, was putting up the last shutter. Relieved, she cruised through downtown. The streets were mostly empty, businesses in The Commons were closed, tables and chairs taken in, sheets of plywood covered the windows and doors, some with previous hurricane names crossed out in red spray paint and "GO AWAY HENRY" below them. She pulled over and texted her mom that The Pour House was boarded up, and they were safe. She knew her mom would have to drive forty minutes into town for Wi-Fi, but if she was worried enough about Henry, she'd do that.

Then she video-called Kittie.

Kittie smiled into the phone. "I heard. Cat 2. We're packing up the snacks and the critters now to head to Paul's."

Mila smiled back, relief loosening the tension in her chest she didn't realize she had. "Thanks, Kittie. I really don't know what we'd do without you."

She chuckled. "A worry for another day. Your kiddo wants to say hi." The screen moved at a dizzying speed and then Harper's face filled it. "Hi, Mom. Grandma said I can bring Iggy to Dad's. And she made peanut butter cookies for Oscar and Max. Are you coming to meet us there?"

She would like nothing more. "I don't know, honey. Right now I have to work, and I don't know when I'll be done."

Her eyes glistened with unshed tears, but she nodded bravely. "Okay. I understand." She glanced behind her. "Don't tell Grandma I told, but I think she's scared."

Mila's heart ached in her chest. She always felt like she was being pulled in two different directions, but it was at times like these when that pull was so strong toward her daughter, to run to her and hold her to keep her safe, that it almost won out over her oath to protect and serve Edgewater. These times, when her job conflicted with being there for Harper, were the only times she second-guessed her career choice. She, too, put on a brave face. "Well, tell Grandma Kittie that Daddy's house is safe, and Oscar won't let anything happen to her."

As if he heard his name, Oscar's muzzle appeared, and he licked Harper's cheek. She wrapped her arm around his head and kissed him between the eyes. When she looked back at the screen, her dimples had appeared. "We won't let anything happen to Oscar, either."

Thank God for dogs. "Hey, did you get your peanut butter and jelly?"

She moved the phone so Mila could see into the kitchen. "Yep. Grandma's packing it now. And my M&M's. She got me the giant bag."

"Did she? Well, don't make yourself sick eating the whole bag." When Harper crossed her heart and smiled mischievously, Mila smiled back. "All right. I have to go but I'll call you later. Love you to the moon and back."

"Me, too." She blew a kiss and then was gone.

Mila stared at the black screen for a moment, listening to the sound of the windshield wipers, letting a wave of sadness pass through her. Then she got her head back in the investigation. Before she took off, she checked the DMV for the car registered to the Burns. No accidents on record. That only meant it was possible they didn't call the police or run it through their insurance if they did have an accident.

When she left The Commons, she drove over to check on Charlie and Rose. As she rolled slowly down the street, she saw Aiden at the house four doors down, also wearing his raincoat and huddled beneath the porch overhang. He was talking to someone inside. She hoped he would get something for them to follow up on.

True to his word, the landlord had put up the hurricane shutters on the small house. Charlie opened the door with Rose on her hip. Rose's face was blotchy from crying, and she was chewing on her fist. Charlie didn't look much better.

"Hey, come on in. It's getting nasty out there," Charlie croaked.

Mila glanced around at the opened boxes strewn around the room and the fast-food bag on the counter. With the hurricane shutters covering the windows and just one lamp glowing in the corner, the house looked depressing and dark. "Here, let me take her for a minute." Mila reached out and took Rose, situating the little girl on her own hip. She smelled like sweat and baby lotion. Rose stared up at her with wide eyes and drool dripping off her bottom lip.

"Thanks," Charlie said, collapsing on the sofa beside a pile of books and picture frames not yet in the boxes. She looked younger, dressed in a yellow tank top and gray yoga pants, her face makeup free. She picked up a framed photo beside her. Mila glanced down at it while she patted Rose's back. It was Cara in the hospital bed, smiling wide as she held a newborn Rose swaddled in a blanket. Charlie's eyes shimmered with tears. "Sometimes it hits me so hard that I'll never hear her laugh again, never argue with her again, that I ... I can't breathe. Does it ever get better?"

As if Rose knew they were talking about her mother, she let out a wail.

Mila bounced her on her hip. "It gets... less sharp." She grabbed the box of Cheerios off the counter and used Fayth's trick of scattering them on a blanket for Rose. When Mila sat her on the blanket, the baby stopped crying and concentrated on picking them up with her chubby little hands.

Mila sank into the chair across from Charlie. She didn't want to talk about losing her own sister, though that would probably help Charlie feel less alone. She just didn't have the emotional strength at the moment. "Tell me about her... about your sister. What was she like?"

Charlie began to trace her sister's face beneath the glass. "Infuriating." She pushed the word out on a soft half-sob, half-laugh. "She was so stubborn. Had to do everything her way. She'd never accept help from me. And she was also so kind. She couldn't see the bad in anyone." She glanced up, a spark of anger in her eyes. "Unfortunately." Her gaze rested on Rose and her shoulders fell. "Our parents stayed married until the day they died, but Dad was never around. He traveled for work." She shrugged. "I think he had a secret family somewhere else, but they haven't turned up yet." Mila noticed she didn't seem to be joking. "Anyway, Cara just craved male attention. She wanted to be loved so badly. It ruled her life." She held the photo to her chest and closed her eyes. "She was loved. She just didn't believe it."

Mila watched Rose rocking on her hands and knees, babbling to herself. "Well, at least you can keep Cara alive for her daughter. I'm sure she'll have a million questions about her mom as she grows up."

Charlie took a deep breath in and nodded. "At least I can do that." Still holding the picture to her chest she asked, "Do you have any idea who did this yet?"

"We're getting closer." She wanted to give Charlie something, some sliver of hope. "We've ruled out her ex-boyfriend."

"Really?" Her brows pressed down, eyes narrowing in thought behind wet lashes. "So, maybe it was random. Just some psycho, and she was in the wrong place at the wrong time."

It wasn't. But Mila couldn't say more, so she changed the subject. "What are you going to do with Cara's things?"

Charlie blinked and glanced around at the mess. "Oh, I'll get a small storage unit when the hurricane passes for the things I think Rose will want, like Cara's artwork. There's not much honestly. A ton of books and some clothes I'll take to Goodwill." Her face crumpled. "I guess I need to think about a funeral."

"One day at a time. Right now, we have to get through Henry first."

Rose crawled toward Cara, finished with the Cheerios game. Cara reached down and scooped her up, held her close and pressed her cheek against the baby's brown curls. "We'll get through this together," she whispered.

Mila's phone buzzed. She pulled it out. It was a text from Aiden:

Where r you

Cara's place

Good. Come 3 doors down on the left. Have something.

Mila said her goodbyes, told her to call if she needed anything and walked briskly down to the house, pulling her jacket tighter around herself. Gusts were whipping the palm trees back and forth, and the rain was coming down in sheets.

A beer-bellied man in his late sixties let her in and led her to where Aiden was seated at the kitchen table, staring at a laptop screen. The rest of the table was covered in hurricane supplies.

"What do you have?" Mila asked, standing behind him and leaning over his shoulder.

He tapped the screen. "This is from this gentleman's ring camera, a little before midnight on Saturday." The video was grainy shades of gray, an empty street, the palm trees swaying slightly. Then a car rolled by, no lights on. Aiden paused it on the frame where the whole left side of the car was visible. "This is the only angle we get, no license plate but it's a light-colored car. Possibly white. Lights off."

"That's definitely suspicious and in our time frame. Maybe the house across the street captured the other side, and we can see if there's front-end damage."

The man scratched his stomach. "Right across the street in the green house, them are the Westons. Snowbirds, so not here." He pointed with his can of Bud Light. "But try the purple house. Lorelei is home."

"Thanks." Aiden handed him a card. "Mind emailing that footage to me?"

"Not at all. Y'all stay safe out there now."

Lorelei's frizzy dyed-pink hair was being held back by a 1980's rainbow headband. A sheen of sweat covered her face, her hand perched on her narrow hip. "Yes?"

"Sorry to bother you, Ma'am." Mila and Aiden both showed her their badges and introduced themselves. "I see you have a ring doorbell camera. We're investigating the death of Cara Anderson and was wondering if we might take a look at your footage from Saturday night around midnight?"

Her face telegraphed disappointment. "I'm real sorry detectives but I can only see live feed, I don't pay for the service where it records anything."

They asked her a few more questions, including if she'd seen a suspicious white car and when she had nothing for them, they went opposite ways, canvassing the whole street, knocking on doors. Most people were home because of the storm. Unfortunately, the only other house that had a recording caught the same side of the light-colored car. They left cards on the few houses that didn't answer the door with *please call me* scribbled on the back. Hopefully, the owners would find them before Henry blew them away.

When they met back up, it was almost eleven, they were wet to the bone, frustrated and feeling the pressure of time running out as the gusts ramped up.

As they were contemplating the next step, both got a text from the captain. Mila fought the wind and held her hair out of her face to read it: *return to the station asap.* "Hopefully Matt found something," Mila said. "See you there."

Her wipers were on high, the wind rocking trees and her SUV as she drove back to the station. It'd been a wet summer and the ground was saturated, so the roads were also already starting to accumulate water.

Once safely indoors, she filled up her mug with lukewarm coffee from the breakroom, threw it in the microwave and then joined the others in the conference room. Her hair and slacks were wet and clinging to her body, so the air-conditioning felt like it was seeping into her bones. She shivered and clutched the heated mug.

Matt had parked his wheelchair in front of the whiteboard, a grim look on his face as he stared at something in a folder.

Frank filed in last, his face gaunt, wiping the rain from his glasses with a napkin. He shook his head at Captain Bartol. "No luck on the wine," he announced as he blew out a deep breath and fell into a chair.

"All right," Captain Bartol said. "It was worth a shot. After this, I need you on the hotline I had set up for the press conference. We need to monitor it for tips as long as the phones are working. Hopefully, someone saw something."

Frank gave her a half-hearted salute.

"What's up, Matt?" Aiden asked. He had apparently noticed the uncharacteristic dark mood, also.

Matt looked up at them. "I finished the background check on Pastor Burns's family. They all check out except for Santos Rosales."

"I just spoke to him a few hours ago," Mila said, surprised. She was usually a good judge of character. "He seemed like a nice kid."

Matt shifted in his wheelchair. "Well, he isn't who he says he is. His real name is Jorge Molina and he's not sixteen, he's twenty-three." He slid a folder onto the table so they could check out the report for themselves. "Apparently, he's a Honduran immigrant who crossed in Mexico, unbeknown to anyone, he had used his friend's name and was taken to a U.S. Department of Health and Human Services shelter as an unaccompanied minor. That was two years ago. He was placed with Pastor Burns as his sponsor sixteen months ago."

Captain Bartol crossed her arms after she passed the folder to Frank, digesting the new information. "So, it's possible Pastor Burns isn't aware of his real identity."

"Possible." Matt held up another stapled report. "And there's something else. The Burns's address before coming to Edgewater four years ago was in Tampa." He tossed the report on the table. "I'm not sure how that fits, but it seems like too much of a coincidence."

Mila scooped it up and skimmed it. She passed it to Aiden and drummed her fingertips on the table. "I just don't see how this connects to our vic. If they left Tampa four years ago, no one in the family could be the reason she moved here. They do have a white Toyota Corolla which looks like the car in the Ring camera footage, but, one, it's a popular car, and, two, Cara's coworker mentioned she felt stalked in Tampa right before she moved. Their car would've been in Edgewater. Plus, there's no record of an accident. I checked."

"Unless someone drove it to Tampa to follow Cara. There are four licensed drivers in that household," Matt said.

"And they could've got the damage fixed with cash in the last few months," Frank said.

Captain Bartol agreed and then added, "I'll get an arrest warrant for Mr. Molina and have patrol pick him up. I.C.E. probably won't be able to take custody until after the storm passes, so we'll have time to have a long chat with him." She turned to Matt. "Anything else? What about the journal?"

"Still working on cracking the passcode."

"Oh, got something." Aiden was scrolling on his phone. "HydeMe just came through with the IP Address. Matt, I'm forwarding it to you."

Matt gave him a thumbs up. "Hopefully I can get the service provider to move that quickly."

Sixteen

Patrol had brought in Jorge Molina and he was sitting in an interview room, chin to his chest. Mila and Aiden had their chairs pulled together, watching him on the monitor. He was still in the soaking wet T-shirt, but no hat. His chin-length, wavy black hair was also wet and wind-blown.

"He does look young for his age. It's possible the Burns's don't know his real story." Mila folded her arms over her stomach, which had started to growl loudly.

Aiden must've noticed because he went to his desk and came back with a baggie of dried fruit and nuts. He held it out to her. "So, how do you want to do this?"

"Thanks. I have a rapport established with him, so I'll go in first." She popped a handful of the sweet and salty snack in her mouth. As she thought about her strategy, she noticed her damp socks were uncomfortable. She'd have to grab dry ones from her locker. After swallowing and taking a sip of water, she said, "We need to get a hair sample from Jorge to compare to the one found on our vic. Let's see how he reacts to that request." She stood, taking one more mouthful of fruit and nuts to hopefully satisfy her growling stomach, then handed him back the baggie.

Aiden dumped some of the snack into his palm and nodded. "Let me know if you need me in there."

Mila stopped in the breakroom, poured a coffee, then headed to the interview room. After stowing her Glock in the gun locker outside, she walked in and set the coffee in front of the distraught young man. He didn't look up. The sour smell of his sweat permeated the small room.

She slid into the chair across the small table and folded her hands. "How you holding up, Jorge?"

He startled, glanced up at her. Maybe at the use of his real name? He probably hadn't heard it spoken since he'd been in the US. His eyes were bloodshot. His voice cracked when he whispered, "I'm sorry I lie."

Mila nodded, gave him a sympathetic smile. "I have to let you know this interview is being video and audio recorded." She pulled out a sheet of paper and read him his Miranda rights. Even as a non-US citizen, the rights still applied. "Do you understand?"

"Yes."

She pushed the paper across the table with a pen. "Please sign the bottom." She waited until he was finished. "So, why don't you help me understand why you came to the US under your friend's name?"

He shifted uncomfortably in the chair and choked out, "*Maras.*" The word sent a shiver through his body. He wrapped his arms tightly around his middle and made eye contact. "Gangs. After Hurricane Eta, my family's home was lost. Everything buried in mud." He made the sign of the cross over his body. "My family, we had a small coffee farm. The rains spoiled the coffee beans. There is no more money to start over. Still, the gangs came to take what little food we had. I tried to fight. If they see me again, I will be dead. You cannot send me back for my mother to bury me." His body began to shake uncontrollably.

Mila understood. Desperation was motivation. She pushed the warm coffee toward him. "I'll be right back." A few minutes later, she returned with a blanket and draped it over his shoulders, though she wasn't sure the shaking was from being cold.

He looked up at her with both suspicion and gratitude. "*Gracias.*"

When she sat back down, she sighed. "I won't lie to you, Jorge. I have no control over you going back to Honduras. I.C.E. will be handling that. Do you understand?"

His eyes grew glassy with a sheen of unshed tears, but he nodded.

Mila studied him. She still felt her initial instinct about him was right, that he was a good kid. But she could be wrong. "What I do have control over is if you also will be charged with murder here in the States."

His head jerked up. "Murder?" He began to shake his head. "Murder who?"

"Cara Anderson."

He pulled the blanket tighter around his shoulder, his head shaking vigorously. "No, no. I don't murder Cara Anderson."

"Then you wouldn't mind giving us a hair sample? We found a hair on her body and we could rule you out if it doesn't match."

He sat back in the chair and nodded. "Yes. You take my hair."

Mila watched him. He was an open book and seemed relieved to be able to give this evidence. Or was it all an act? She glanced up at the camera and nodded. "Okay, good. So where were you Sunday night between nine and one in the morning?"

His teeth scraped his lower lip as he glanced up at the camera. "At home until eleven then I was out."

Mila raised an eyebrow and waited for him to continue. When he didn't, she prompted. "Were you out alone? With someone?"

His gaze bounced off hers. "Out alone."

Mila tapped the table in front of him to get his attention. "Jorge, this is serious. No more lies."

He opened his mouth to say something and then snapped it shut.

Mila eyed him as he seemed to fold in on himself. She had to be careful so he didn't shut down. He had nothing to gain by talking to her. In his mind, he already had a death sentence waiting for him back in Honduras.

She changed directions. "Did Pastor Burns or anyone in the family know your real identity?"

A soft moan escaped him. The pain of hurting a family that had trusted him, no doubt. "No. They are good people. I tried my best to be good to them, too."

The door opened and Officer Sally Simms came in with a black leather bag. She nodded at Mila and then explained to Jorge what she would be doing. They stayed silent while she worked, plucking and combing hairs from various parts of Jorge's scalp and dropping them into separate envelopes. When she left, Jorge still had his head hanging, like it was too heavy to lift.

Mila asked, "Is there anything I can get you. Are you hungry?"

He only shook his head slightly, still not looking at her.

She had to move away from Cara's murder, get him talking again. "Let's talk about the Toyota in the garage. Everyone in the family shares that car?"

He finally lifted his head. Then he removed the blanket from his shoulders and rubbed his face like he was waking up from a deep sleep. There was some color to it finally. "Yes."

"Was it ever involved in an accident? Have front-end damage that was repaired?"

His eyes held hers steady for the first time. Determination burned in them. "Not that I know of."

For the first time, Mila didn't believe him. "Are you protecting someone, Jorge?" She watched his jaw muscles tighten. She took that as a yes. "I understand the loyalty to the family who took you in, gave you a chance at a life here.

But a girl has had her life ripped away. A baby has lost her mother. Neither of them deserved that."

His words were more of an outburst. "Of course, I know this." He closed his eyes and then opened them, the sparks of anger beginning to ignite. "No one deserves a violent death."

Mila nodded. *Just how angry could he get? Angry enough to kill?* "I'll be back in a few minutes." She left the room. He was beginning to thaw emotionally, his situation was sinking in. She would let that build, then maybe he would make a mistake and say something he didn't want to say.

She met Aiden and Captain Bartol back in the bullpen where they had been watching the interview on a monitor.

"Officer Simms is running the hair samples over to the lab. They can at least compare the two samples to see if they're a match before sending them for DNA analysis," Captain Bartol said.

"What do you think so far? Theories?" Aiden asked.

Mila lowered herself into her chair, thinking about everything they knew so far. "What if Cara found out that he wasn't who he said he was? Threatened to tell the family or authorities? Or blackmailed him, and that's where the cash came from in her bank account. Though we're still missing the connection of how Cara knew them before she moved here." She rubbed her temples in frustration.

"That's a big missing piece." Captain Bartol sipped from a cup with a tea bag. Her eyes filled with skepticism. "On the other hand, blackmail would be motive. And Jorge also had opportunity since he admitted he was out after eleven but won't say where or with whom. Though I'm not sure where he'd get that kind of money."

Mila checked her FitBit. It was almost 1 p.m. They only had about six hours before they'd have to lock everything down until Henry passed. The rain was beating against the window in a steady, drumming rhythm now. Six hours was not enough to solve this thing, but they had to try. It would be chaos after the storm passed with no phone service, no electricity. Who knew when they could get back to work.

Matt appeared in the doorway, holding up a piece of paper. This time there was an excitement to his energy. "I got something, guys." He rolled in and handed it to Mila. "The ISP came through with the contact information for the IP address."

Mila and Aiden read it together and then shared a nod. "That's the Burns's home address," she said. They glanced at the monitor. Jorge had his head resting on his forearms on the table. "We've gotta break him before I.C.E. picks him up." She leaned back to address the captain. "How long did they say the hair comparison would take?"

Captain Bartol rubbed her forehead. She rarely showed signs of stress. This seemed to be one of them. "About an hour."

Mila turned to Aiden. "Okay. Let's both go in." She squeezed Matt's shoulder on the way out. "Thanks."

Mila and Aiden had one goal now: to wear down Jorge, get him to confess. If there was something to confess.

Aiden slapped the paper with the Burns's address on the table in front of Jorge. "We know you texted Cara a few hours before she was killed to arrange the meet-up at the beach." Jorge's brows pressed down, but he stayed silent. "Did she discover your real identity? Was she blackmailing you? Did you give her cash for her silence? Maybe you ran out of cash so she was going to the police."

"Are you a religious man, Jorge?" Mila asked.

His eyes darted back and forth between them. "Yes."

Mila made a calculated decision to reveal a fact to him that the public didn't know yet. She needed to see his reaction. "Is that why you carved 'forgive me' on Cara's body? To ask God for forgiveness for what you did? Do you think he forgives you?"

Jorge's mouth dropped open and he froze for a split second. "Yes... I mean no, he does not forgive me." He ran his hands roughly through his hair then dropped them heavily on the table. "Because I have done nothing wrong."

"You don't think taking a life is wrong?" Aiden asked.

"Of course." Jorge's voice rose and cracked. "It's wrong."

"This is a heavy burden to carry, Jorge. Eventually, it will break you, destroy your life. It's better to just get the truth out there and deal with the consequences than let it eat you alive."

Tears flowed down his face as his shoulders fell. "Don't you understand? I am already a dead man."

Mila tore a sheet out of her notebook and pushed it across the table with her pen. "If you really feel that way, it won't do any harm to you to write an apology to Cara's family. To her daughter. I think God would approve of that."

The door cracked open, and Captain Bartol stuck her head in, jerked it to signal she needed them.

Aiden tapped the notebook paper. "We'll be right back, Jorge. You work on that letter."

When they closed the door behind them, Captain Bartol sighed. "The hair comparison was not a match."

Mila and Aiden stared at her in stunned silence. The only sound was the rattling of the air conditioning and the rain pounding the roof.

After they recovered, Mila shook her head. "So, someone else in that house must have sent the text."

Aiden raked a hand over his face and blew out a breath. "Okay, let's think. Now that we have proof the text came from the Burns's address, can't we get a warrant for a hair sample for the two other men there?"

Captain Bartol had her hands in her slacks pocket. Her shoulders raised. "I don't know. There's no motive for the other two. We have to find something else that links Cara to somebody in that family."

Mila glanced back at the closed door. "We still need to find out where Jorge was that night. He might not have been the one that killed Cara, but maybe he was involved. Maybe he helped and is covering for one of the others in the family."

Captain Bartol glanced at the ceiling as a vicious gust of wind rattled the vents. "We need to talk to both Pastor Burns and Julian. I'm afraid if we bring them here, they'll be stuck during the hurricane, but it might be worth it."

"We still have a few hours. But if they do get stuck here, this is a safe place to ride it out," Aiden said.

Mila didn't disagree. "Pastor Burns told me he was sick that night... food poisoning or something. I can at least verify that with his family. It will give me an excuse to talk to everyone again. See if I can shake something loose. If not, I'll ask him and Julian to come in. And if I can get them to agree to a hair sample, we can use that as leverage to get a confession."

"If it's a match." Captain Bartol checked her watch. "Okay, go. Let's divide and conquer. Aiden, you stay on Jorge. See if you can find out where he was that night. Mila, go talk to the Burns family, but keep an eye on the time. You have roughly five hours before you need to be off the roads and indoors."

Seventeen

Mila rapped hard on the front door. The rain was now lashing her back, her pants were soaked through once again and water ran down into her shoes. Good thing she never got to change into dry clothes. A powerful gust blew her forward and she braced herself against the doorframe.

"Detective?" Pastor Burns's eyes widened. "Come in." He moved aside and shut the door quickly behind her. "Is this about Santos? Is he okay? The police wouldn't tell us anything when they picked him up."

The whole family was gathered in the small living room and seemed startled to see her. Good.

"Yes, in part." Mila removed her dripping raincoat and left it on the tile by the door along with her wet messenger bag. Their gazes flitted to her duty belt. At times like these she was just a woman with a scar, a badge, and a gun and that was okay. She glanced at each one of them, noting their demeanor. They all seemed unsettled, but that could be from the storm. Lionel was the only one she couldn't get a read on. He was snoring in his wheelchair in the corner, a knitted Afghan blanket over his knees.

"Please have a seat." Pastor Burns motioned for Jemma to get up from the chair Mila had sat in before. Jemma smacked her brother's feet off the sofa and claimed the space. On the coffee table were candles, flashlights and a bowl of popcorn.

"You're soaking wet," Lynnie said, setting her knitting down on the side table and quickly standing. "Can I get you a hot cup of tea?"

"That would be lovely, thank you." Mila took the chair and purposefully let the silence grow, spreading into discomfort.

Pastor Burns lowered himself next to Jemma and cleared his throat. He was in sweatpants and a white T-shirt with the church's logo on the front. "What's going on? Is Santos in some kind of trouble?"

"Yes, unfortunately. Let's wait until your wife gets back and I'll tell you all together." She moved her attention to Jemma's brother, who she hadn't had a conversation with yet. "Julian, right?"

Julian's dark gaze flicked up from his phone. It was full of mistrust. He and Jemma had the same eyes and demeanor. "Yeah."

She let her face relax into a smile. "Are you and Jorge close?"

His confusion showed in the tight pinch between his brows. He glanced at the pastor questioningly. When he got no answer there, he turned his attention back to Mila. "Who's Jorge?"

Mila searched everyone's face in the room. No guilt, no dishonesty. Just genuine curiosity. They didn't know.

Lynnie returned and handed her a cup and saucer, the teabag still steeping in the steaming water, a packet of sugar on the side.

"Thank you." Mila waited until Lynnie returned to her seat and then addressed them all. "Unfortunately, Santos's real name is Jorge Molina and he's not sixteen, he's twenty-three."

She let them process that. They were sharing stunned glances and Jemma whispered a quiet, "Oh my God," which got a disapproving look from Lynnie.

"Are you sure?" Pastor Burns's voice was hoarse with emotion. "He's such a good person. I just can't imagine that kind of deception from him."

Mila nodded. "He had a good reason." She told them about the gang that would kill him if he went back to Honduras. A heavy gust made the house crack and groan. She glanced up at the ceiling. This house was definitely built before 2002, when the new hurricane codes went into place. She hoped they had updated it and added the hurricane clips.

Lynnie's voice brought her back to the reason she was here. "Is there anything we can do to keep him here?" Her lip quivered, a pale hand was pressed over her heart.

"Honestly, I don't think so. But that's not our jurisdiction. I.C.E. will be taking custody of him once the storm passes." Appropriately named, she thought to herself as she watched the chilling effect those three letters had on the family.

"Can we at least see him?" Pastor Burns asked.

"Possibly, if you get to the station before the agents show up, I don't think there would be any harm in letting you all say goodbye." Mila took a sip of the tea, enjoying the trail of heat it blazed down her throat. This would be a good way to get them to the station, too. Once there, it would be easier to get each of them in an interview room.

She would save most of the questions for when they were separated, but there was one thing she could ask now. "Pastor Burns, you had mentioned you'd got food poisoning the night Cara was killed?"

His face was ashen, and he still looked dazed from the news about Jorge. His gaze was slow to meet hers. "Oh, yes. I did."

Mila glanced at Lynnie. "Can you verify that?"

Lynnie was pressing a tissue under her eyes. "Well, yes. He was pretty sick. Vomiting and sweating and barely able to move from the bed. Santos..." she stumbled over the name, "he stayed with me until around eleven, when he went to bed. We were feeding Collin ice chips and praying. We were very concerned. I even called the doctor's emergency number, and the nurse called me back."

So, Jorge was at least telling the truth about being home until eleven. "Do you mind if I see that call log?" Mila asked.

"Oh," Lynnie glanced around. "Sure, let me get my phone."

Mila's gaze settled on Julian, who now seemed to be texting. *Where was he that night?* She had to be careful. She didn't want to question him right now and scare him off from coming to the station. She had a much better shot at getting him to talk under the pressure of an interview there. What she needed right now was a hair sample. She still had time to run it to the lab if a tech was still there. "Excuse me, I need to make a call."

She moved back to the front door and called the forensic lab. Brooklyn picked up. She agreed to wait for Mila if she could get there within the next thirty minutes. Perfect.

"Here you go." Lynnie handed Mila her cell phone with the call log pulled up for the day of Cara's murder. The call to the doctor at 9:14 that evening checked out.

"Thanks." She handed the phone back and turned toward the pastor. "I need to ask one more thing to clear you and Julian from any suspicion in Cara's death."

Julian's head jerked up. "What?"

Pastor Burns reached over Jemma and placed a calming hand on his knee. "Of course, whatever you need. We have nothing to hide."

"Thank you." Mila unzipped her water-logged messenger bag and pulled out a pair of gloves and her kit: a pair of tweezers, a comb and evidence envelopes. "I'm going to take a sample from each of the five areas of your scalp, which I'll then take to the forensic tech. She'll see if they're a match with the hair sample we've pulled from Cara's body, so we'll know in a few hours. I'll be gentle, I promise."

After she collected the samples, she addressed the whole family. "You all have a few hours before we would suggest being off the roads. If you want to make sure you see Jorge, I can call and clear a visit with Chief Bartol."

Pastor Burns nodded. "We would like that."

"Give me a half hour and then head over."

※

The roads were clear of traffic. Most people were already hunkered down wherever they were going to ride out the storm. So, despite the absolutely terrible visibility and the water already building up and causing a hydroplaning hazard, she made it to the crime lab, dropped off the sample and was back to the station in forty minutes.

Captain Bartol walked with Mila through the hall. "The family is in the media room. I told them they can visit one at a time, gives you time to talk to each one individually, too. Hopefully we can keep them here until Brooklyn gets back to us with the results of the hair samples."

"Frank get anything good on the tipline yet?" Mila asked.

"A few leads we'll have to chase down after the storm, but I don't think they'll go anywhere." She opened the door and whispered, "I'll put Jorge back in an interview room for the visits. That way we can record the conversations." Mila nodded and walked in.

The room held four long tables, chairs, a podium for holding press conferences and two monitors on the front wall. Against the back wall were piles of sleeping bags, backpacks and coolers. They would move the tables against the walls this evening for patrol and first responders to shelter here.

Mila addressed Pastor Burns after taking inventory of the family. "Jemma didn't want to come?"

He had his hands clasped in front of him like he'd been praying. "She's pretty angry with Santos...I mean Jorge, and she feels like she doesn't know him at all. She offered to stay home with Lionel and make sure he takes his medication."

She should've known Lionel wasn't going to come. How incapacitated was he? Maybe she should've tried to talk to him at the house. "I see. So who wants to go first?"

Lynnie stood, chin up, and smoothed down her blue flowered shirt. "I will."

"After you." Mila led her into the interview room where Jorge sat, head down in defeat. Lynnie immediately went over and wrapped her arms around his shoulders. "It'll be okay," she said soothingly. "We understand why you did it and forgive you. God doesn't give us more than we can handle."

Jorge's shoulders began to shake as he quietly sobbed in her arms.

Mila closed the door and moved into the bullpen where Aiden was standing, watching them on the monitor, arms folded. They watched as Lynnie slid into the chair across from him, clutching his hands and began to pray.

"I'm going to start with the brother, Julian. In case we run out of time," Mila said.

"Go ahead, I'll keep an eye on Jorge."

Julian reluctantly went with her to an interview room. Pastor Burns had to encourage him to go, reminding him he had nothing to hide. Mila hoped that was true.

Eighteen

Mila wanted to ease into the questions. Get him comfortable. Right now he had his arms crossed protectively and a suspicious gleam in his eyes. Maybe that was just a teenage thing, but maybe it was something more sinister. "Your sister told me how rough you two had it before the Burns's adopted you. How you'd survived abusive foster homes and been separated. She feels like the Burns's saved her life. Do you feel that way, too?"

His eyes softened but also flashed with surprise. "I do, yeah."

Mila offered him an understanding smile. "How do you feel about Jorge lying to your family then?"

He shifted in the chair and shrugged. "I understand why he did it."

She tried to see his eyes, but he had them cast down. "No hard feelings then?"

"Nah. He was always good to me."

"In what way?"

He licked his lips, his gaze flicking to the camera. He shrugged again.

Interesting. Julian was covering for something. The one thing her gut told her they were lying about for sure was the car. "Who wrecked the Toyota?"

Julian's eyes widened perceptively. "No one. It's fine."

It's fine now. "Look, Julian, you seem to really care about Jorge. If you want to help him out... keep him from being charged with Cara Anderson's murder, you should come clean if you know where he was after he left the house at eleven Friday night."

Julian stared at her, some internal struggle playing out in his facial micro-expressions. Then he closed his eyes and his shoulders dropped. When he opened his eyes, they held something new... defeat. "Sometimes I sneak out my bedroom window. Go hang out, go to a party." He held up his palms. "It's just the Burnes are great to us, but so strict about some things. I just need to be around people my own age sometimes, let loose, ya know?"

"Sure. Makes sense." Mila kept her body relaxed, though every nerve ending was at attention, alert for deception, holding the crumbs he was giving her and comparing them to the pieces of the story she already had. "What time did you leave the house Friday?"

"Around nine. There's this girl... Shelly, we sort of hook up sometimes. But, she was all over this other guy and I wasn't feeling it. I was going to split an Uber with her to get home later, but I wanted to leave early and didn't have the money. So, I texted Santos ... Jorge around eleven and ask him to come get me. And he did."

If Julian didn't even have money for an Uber, it wasn't likely he had a couple grand lying around to give to Cara. Unless he did and now was out of money. "What time did Jorge show up?"

His mouth twisted in thought. "Around midnight, I guess."

"It took him an hour to get to you?" Her tone purposefully dripped with skepticism.

"Yeah." He leaned forward to make his case. "Well, I mean, he had to sneak out and get the car out of the garage without waking up the house. Takes time to roll it to the street before he could start it."

"And then what time did you two get back to the house?"

"A little before twelve-thirty."

Mila tore a sheet from her notebook and pushed it across the table with a pen. "I'm going to need an address for that party, Shelly's name and number and anyone else's contact information you have who was there that night."

He pulled out his phone and started writing down contacts. At one point he glanced up. "He didn't kill Cara, you know. He wouldn't do that."

Mila heard the sincerity in his tone. But how well did he actually know the man who'd been living with them posing as a teenager? Or did Julian know Jorge didn't kill Cara because *he* had? Hopefully, Brooklyn would have the comparison of the hair sample finished soon and they'd be closer to the truth.

Mila walked Julian back to the media room. "You can speak with Jorge next." Then she asked Pastor Barnes to come with her.

She ushered him into a second interview room and sat him at the table. "Be right back."

Moving quickly, she entered the room where Jorge sat alone, his gaze rooted to the table. He hadn't written the apology letter she'd asked him to earlier. *Was that because he wasn't sorry? Or because he didn't do it?*

"Hey." She waited for Jorge to lift his head and held eye contact with him. "Julian has come clean about sneaking out of the house to go to a party Friday night. So, I need you to tell me the truth as well."

He slowly straightened his spine and nodded. A bit of relief surfacing in his eyes. "He asked me to pick him up so I did. He was upset about his girl."

Mila stood over him, arms crossed, invading his space. "And what time did you pick him up?"

He leaned back so he could look up at her. His eyes were red rimmed, his lips were chapped and raw where he'd been picking at the skin. "Around midnight, I think."

"He said he texted you at eleven?"

"Possible. I do not know exactly."

"That's okay. We can check your phone." She leaned down, pressing her hands into the table, her face inches from his. "Why didn't you tell me this when I asked where you were Friday night?"

He dipped his head. "He was drinking. I do not want him to get in trouble."

Mila studied him for a moment before she straightened back up. "Okay, sit tight." She left him alone again.

"What was that about?" Aiden asked, as she entered the bullpen.

She handed him the paper with the contacts from the party. "Julian said he snuck out to go to a party Friday night and Jorge picked him up around midnight. This is the address and contacts. Specifically, a girl named Shelly he says he hooks up with."

Aiden pushed himself out of the chair and grabbed his rain jacket. "Got it. I'll run over to the address and confirm. Roads should still be okay. I can make the calls when we get stuck here later tonight." A heavy object made a loud thwack as it hit the window behind the blinds. His brow raised. "If phone service is still up." Aiden glanced at the address. "Depending on where this address is, Jorge could've had enough time to make a stop at the beach where Cara was before picking up Julian."

Mila shook her head. She really didn't think Jorge had anything to do with Cara's death. "Or Julian could be using Jorge. What if Julian actually snuck out of the house to meet Cara? Killed her, went to the party to have an alibi then called Jorge to get him from that location."

Aiden slipped on the still-damp rain jacket. "I'll see if I can confirm he was there the whole time. What time did he say he arrived?"

"Said he snuck out of the house around nine. Stay dry." Mila smirked.

"Funny."

Mila returned to Pastor Burns and gave him a sympathetic look as she took a seat across from him. "Seems your boys were not where they were supposed to be Friday night."

He blinked and his forehead crinkled with concern. "What do you mean?"

Mila leaned her forearms on the table. "Julian admitted to sneaking out to a party around nine that night then texted Jorge to pick him up around eleven. Jorge got there around midnight and brought him home."

Pastor Burns rubbed a hand roughly over his cheek. "Well, I guess that doesn't surprise me. Julian is a bit of a rebel and doesn't always make the best choices. Jorge is very loyal to the family so yeah... I can see him bailing out Julian." Then his head snapped up. "Oh. If they were out of the house, they no longer have an alibi for Cara's murder." He shook his head. "They are good kids. I really can't see either of them hurting anyone."

But someone in that house did. "What about the car? Did one of them wreck the Corolla?"

He smiled. "Julian." Shook his head. "He had just got his license. Took a turn too fast and hit a light pole. It was still drivable, just some front-end damage. So we decided it would be a good lesson for him to pay for the damage instead of putting it through our insurance and raising our rates. It took him over a year to save up the money, working odd jobs for people. Just got it fixed a few months ago."

The timeframe fit. It could've been the car with the front-end damage Cara thought was following her. Obviously Jorge knew who was responsible, so why did he not want to tell her about a simple accident? He's protective of the family, yes.

Still seems strange. Also, Julian didn't own up to that, either. "Why did you move your family from Tampa four years ago?"

"Well, I was an associate pastor in Tampa. When an opening came up here for a pastor, I applied and got the job."

Mila cocked her head. "An associate pastor?"

The corner of his mouth lifted. "I came to the ministry a bit later in life. Before that I was an insurance salesman. It's a long story, but basically, I needed something more, needed to feel like I was actually making a difference."

She could relate to that. "And do you? Feel like you're making a difference?"

He sighed and leaned back in the chair. "Sometimes, yes. Sometimes I doubt my own path. No one's perfect and the pressure to be a perfect role model gets daunting." His gaze unfocused, his words becoming a whisper. "I'm only human."

Mila was about to latch onto that self-doubt when Captain Bartol stuck her head in the door and motioned for Mila to join her.

"Be right back." She stepped into the hall and shut the door behind her. "What's up?"

Captain Bartol handed Mila a sheet of paper. "The hair sample comparison is back. They'll have to do a DNA test to be sure, but right now enough characteristics are the same to consider it a match for Julian."

Mila stared at the results, finding she was a little surprised, though she shouldn't have been. "All right, put him back in interview room two, I'll go talk to him. By the way, Aiden's gone to the house where Julian said he was at a party that night. I'll text him and let him know about these results. Maybe he can poke some holes in his alibi."

"I'll take care of that for you."

Mila went back into the interview room and stood in front of the table, deciding whether to tell the pastor about the hair sample match. *Would he change his tune about Julian if he knew he could've murdered Cara? Stop protecting him? Maybe.* "We just got word back from the lab. The hair pulled from Cara's body the night she was murdered is a preliminary match with Julian's sample."

He froze. "What does that mean?"

She stood in front of him and held his gaze. "It means we'll do a DNA test to be sure, but it looks like he was there with Cara the night she was murdered."

He shook his head slightly, his face registering shock. A sheen of tears appeared over his brown eyes. "Excuse me. Do you mind if I have a moment to pray?"

If the pastor had previous knowledge Julian that had something to do with Cara's death, he was one hell of an actor. "Of course. Take all the time you need. I'm going to go talk to him now."

Julian had his arms crossed, his leg shaking nervously. The air conditioning vent was closed in this room on purpose, and it was uncomfortably warm. He glared at Mila as she sat down across from him, annoyance pinching the corners of his mouth tight. Under these harsh lights, a scar above his eyebrow shimmered silver. Something her mother always said surfaced: You never know what people have been through, so be kind. Unfortunately, right now, it wasn't Mila's job to be kind. It was her job to uncover the truth.

The sound of the howling winds penetrated the thick wall and the lights flickered. She decided to get right to it. She pushed the piece of paper with the hair sample results in front of him. "The hair sample I took from you is a match to the hair found on Cara's dead body, Julian. Do you want to explain that?"

He dropped his elbows on the table, shoved his hands into the hair at his temples as he stared at the results. When he sat back and looked at her, it wasn't with the fear or panic she'd expected. It was with confusion. "I don't understand."

She studied his demeanor, saw nothing that would indicate deception to her. But that could just mean he felt no guilt and didn't believe he'd get caught.

She held her palms up. "Hey, I'm just trying to help you out here, Julian. Give you a chance to tell the truth. Believe me, it'll go a long way toward good will with the prosecutor." Keeping her tone friendly, she added, "My fellow detective is on his way to the house where you said you were at the party until midnight. He'll find out if you left at any point. Would you like to amend your story?"

"No. I told you the truth." A slight bit of panic widened his eyes. The seriousness of his situation had hit him and sweat beaded above his upper lip. "You think I killed Cara?" He leaned forward, his breathing rate increasing, nostrils flaring. "Look, I barely knew the girl. I wouldn't have any reason to hurt her. I mean, I wouldn't hurt anyone." He smacked his fists on the sides of his temples. "I shouldn't be talking to you. I want to talk to my dad." He suddenly looked like a scared kid instead of a cocky teenager.

Mila leaned forward on the table, closing the gap between them. "Sure, as soon as you tell me the truth, Julian. Let's start with why you lied to me about the car. Your dad told me you were the one who wrecked it, the one who caused that front-end damage."

"The car?" He struggled with the change of subject for a second before a flash of guilt crossed his face. "Oh." He took a sip from the water bottle she'd brought him earlier and wiped his hand across his mouth. What he finally looked at her, he seemed to have made a decision. "Yeah, that's what he thinks. But... it was Jemma. She only had her learner's permit, she got it late you know? She'd never been interested in driving. I don't really know what made her want to start. But she wasn't supposed to be driving without an adult after dark. When she ran off the road and hit the pole, she panicked." His hand moved to press against his chest. "She called me, and I went and drove the car back home, told Dad that I did it."

His open posture and hand on his heart told her he was most likely telling the truth. Mila relaxed back in the chair. "And Jorge knew this, too?"

"Yeah, he would never rat on Jemma." His words caught in his throat. "Isn't there anything you can do to help him? To help him stay here with us?"

Mila reached over and tapped the paper in front of him. "Right now I think you should be worried about yourself, Julian."

Captain Bartol opened the door and waved her out again. Mila tried not to get frustrated, but these interruptions were making it hard to press Julian.

Matt was in the hall with her. He looked up, eyes sparkling with excitement, and handed her a sheet of paper. "I got into the journal. Cara Anderson describes the night she got pregnant with Rose."

Mila blinked as she read and reread the journal passage. Her heart rate kicked up five notches and she had to lean against the wall. "Holy shit."

Nineteen

Mila took a deep breath before she opened the door to the interview room and sank into the chair. She regarded the man across from her, trying to reconcile what she'd just found out with the image he projects to the world. It made no sense. Time to make it make sense.

"You're Rose's father."

A stillness came over him. It reminded her of those nature documentaries when the antelope spots the lion crouched in the grass. His quiet gaze moved from her face to the paper on the table in front of her. A few tense seconds ticked by, and then his shoulders collapsed. He squeezed his eyes shut and gave a curt nod. When his eyes opened, defeat darkened them. They were the eyes of a man who knew his life was about to be changed forever.

"Yes," he whispered.

"Not only are you Rose's father, but you raped her. You raped Cara." Her voice trembled with undisguised anger.

His brows pressed down. "No. No, that's... that's not true."

Mila folded her arms and sat back. "Okay, tell me your version of what happened that night. Before you begin, I need to read you your rights." She read him his Miranda rights and had him sign the bottom. "And be aware this conversation is being recorded." *Would he invoke his right to a lawyer?* It was always a risk at this point and if he was smart, he would. She waited. He didn't.

Pastor Burns glanced up at the ceiling, like he was asking for God's help and then he began. "I volunteered for Christ Fellowship Church's Domestic Violence program in Tampa. Or at least I did when I lived there. The night I met Cara, Pastor Murray had an emergency and had to go out of town, so he'd called me and asked me to fill in for him. I drove up to Tampa... not knowing I would be tested and fail."

That explains why his name wasn't on the list the Church gave Mila. He wasn't supposed to be there that night. She silently waited for him to continue.

"Cara came in with a freshly swelling knot on her cheek, crying hysterically, scared out of her mind. She was convinced her boyfriend was going to kill her. I looked up her file and she'd only been there twice before so there was no plan to get her out yet. I took her to the pastor's office and let her lie down on the couch. Got an icepack for her cheek. Some hot tea." His gaze unfocused. "She really opened up to me. After an hour or so of talking... I mean, really talking, she was so warm and bright and just a kind soul who didn't deserve the abuse she was enduring, she sat up and wrapped her arms around me. I was stunned. But..." he raised his hands in a helpless gesture, "I accepted the embrace and held her because it was obviously what she needed in that moment. Human contact. To feel protected. But then, she lifted her head from my shoulder and pressed her lips against mine." He reached up and touched his lips, remembering. "The heat and adrenaline that went through my body was like a fire. It consumed all rational thought. I suppose I justified letting the kiss deepen, and continuing the contact... that she needed this, not me. That she needed to see that men weren't all bad, that we could provide love and pleasure, not just pain."

Mila's anger bubbled in her chest. She took a purposeful breath and bit her tongue.

"It was like reality fell away. We made love right there on the couch." He finally forced himself to make eye contact with Mila, his eyes glassy with tears, pain and guilt. "I can see now that it was wrong. How could something so wrong feel so right?" He collapsed. "And then, of course, God made me a father. Something that I'd wanted for so long, my own child. Something that Lynnie and I hadn't been able to accomplish. Why with Cara? I don't know. But it was both a blessing and a curse."

An image came unbidden of a rose in Mila's mind, both velvety petals and sharp thorns. Had Cara given Rose her name for that reason? Did Cara think of the baby as both a blessing and a curse? Mila would never know. "You gave Cara the money to move to Edgewater? The four thousand and then another three thousand when she got to Edgewater?"

He glanced up, seemingly surprised she knew about that. "Yes. I helped them move here. I wanted to watch Rose grow up. Be a part of her life in whatever way I could."

Mila's tone was harsher than she meant it to be. "Just not as a father?"

He didn't seem to take offense. "No. That would've destroyed Lynnie. Can you imagine? She wanted us to have a child so badly. We tried so hard. To know God gave another woman my child? It would have destroyed her."

Mila wanted to point out that it was his act of violence that created a child, not God's magic wand. She gritted her teeth. "I don't think you give your wife enough credit."

"Probably not." He sighed. "Also, I didn't want to ruin our church. Erase all the good we've done. A scandal like this, people would lose faith, leave. No butts in the seats means no money in the offering plates. I'd lose my job and displace the rest of our family." He shook his head. "This was the only way."

Looks like Cara and Rose's well-being was an afterthought. After the offering plates. Does he hear himself? "And is that how Cara felt, too?"

He shifted uncomfortably in the chair. "At first she did. But after Rose was born, she decided she wanted real child support, and she didn't want to hide Rose. She wanted her to know I was her father."

Mila wondered if that decision was born from anger. After all, she had a new human being to take care of, a new trauma to deal with and Pastor Burns was just living his life like it had never happened. *Did Cara want him to have consequences? Want his wife to know about Rose? If so, was that what got her killed?*

"Okay, Pastor. That's your version. Now let me read you Cara's." Mila cleared her throat and picked up the journal entry. "Yesterday was the worst night of my life. Joey came home from work drunk and in a really bad mood. I was working on a special art piece to give to my manager for her birthday so I lost track of time and didn't have any dinner ready for him. I said I'd make something real quick, but he wasn't having it. His eyes went black like they do when he loses control. He picked up the petrified wood I'd found on the beach and hit me in the face. Hard. I thought I was going to black out. He said go get him a beer and when he went in the bathroom, I ran out the door. Took the bus to Christ Fellowship Church. I didn't know what else to do. I had to stay away until he sobered up. There was a different pastor there. Pastor Burns. He was younger, real nice. Got me ice for my face and let me cry for an hour in the office. We talked and for the first time I felt like maybe I could leave Joey. Like maybe they could help me get away. He was so confident and so caring. The relief and the hope were overwhelming, and I made a mistake. I kissed him. I mean, I know he's a pastor and all, but that's the only way I knew how to show him my gratitude, thank him for his kindness. I thought he'd understand that's what it was. But he took it the wrong way. I didn't want it to go any further. But when he deepened the kiss and began lying me back on the couch, I froze. He started removing my clothes and I tried to pull them back on. Tried to push him away but my arms wouldn't move. My throat was closed up. My heart was racing so hard, I thought I'd die of a heart attack. All I could do was stare at the tiny spider on the ceiling above me. At one point I felt like I was floating on the ceiling with it, just watching what was happening below. His body suffocating me. Then it was over. He pulled a blanket over me and told me to get some rest. When he closed the door behind him, I could finally move. I was shaking so hard and I needed to throw up, but I managed to get my clothes back on. I snuck back out the front doors without seeing him again. I feel so dirty. Why did I kiss him? How can God even look at me now? There's no way I can go back to that church for help."

Mila glanced up. Pastor Burns had his hands cupped over his mouth, his eyes closed. Eventually, he dropped his hands to his lap, his face pale. "Dear God." His head fell back and he stared at the ceiling. "How did I get that so wrong? I made her life so much worse."

"She was a vulnerable young woman. I can't imagine thinking sex with her in that state was a good idea. But, hey..." Mila made herself take a calming breath. "We're all human, right." Her voice was edged with sarcasm. "Tell me about the last conversation you had with Cara."

His whole body sagged like the weight of what he'd just learned was too heavy to bear. "It was the night she died. We talked on the phone."

"A burner phone?"

"No, I used the house phone to call. I wasn't worried about it because Lynnie would call her from that number to confirm appointments. On my personal cell phone, I had an app that we could text privately."

Mila made a note of that. "Go on."

"I was actually supposed to meet Cara at the beach that night to talk about the child support payments and telling my family about Rose. I agreed to meet, but I was really hoping to talk her out of it. I just… I never got the chance."

So that explains why Cara was at the beach that night. She thought she was finally getting what she wanted, the truth to come out. "You never got a chance to talk to her because you got sick and had to cancel."

Pastor Burns was twisting his gold wedding band slowly on his finger. "Yes. Well, actually I never did get a chance to text her back and cancel. If I had, she'd probably still be alive. Another sin I have to atone for."

Mila dismissed his guilt. It wasn't her problem. "Okay. So, Cara went there still expecting you to show. You didn't… but someone did." She needed a moment to think about what he'd just told her and where to go from here. She gathered her notes and stood. "Can I get you some water? Coffee? Stale snack from the vending machine?"

"Water would be appreciated." His voice was gruff with emotion. He suddenly looked panicked as he added, "And please, don't tell Lynnie yet. Let me tell her."

"Sorry, I can't promise that. Be right back." She walked down the hall and back into the bullpen where Captain Bartol and Matt had been watching.

"Wow." Captain Bartol drew out the word as Mila stood beside them and stared at the pastor on the monitor. She had a pencil shoved behind her ear and her short, red hair looked wind-blown. "His alibi is solid from nine to one?"

Mila bit the inside of her cheek. "Yeah. I mean, the wife confirmed he was home and really sick. She even showed me the call to and from the doctor's office."

Matt held a steaming cup of noodles in one hand and a plastic spoon in the other. "Maybe the wife found out about

Rose and was in on it. Helped him set up that alibi so they could get rid of Cara together?"

"Anything's possible. But why kill Cara? She's not really the problem. Rose is." Mila watched Pastor Burns. He had his eyes closed. He seemed to be praying. Was he praying for forgiveness? For help not getting caught?

"But Cara is the only one who knows the truth about Rose besides him. Remember the pastor's name isn't on the birth certificate. Get rid of her and their problem is solved," Captain Bartol said. "Plus, who has the stomach to kill a baby."

"Okay." Mila turned toward them. "We still have the issue of the hair sample matching Julian. So, what if Pastor Burns sent Julian there to "take care" of Cara that night? What if they were working together?"

"What if they were all working together? The family does seem very loyal to each other." Captain Bartol nodded. "Let's go with that. Go back in to talk to Julian. I'll take the good pastor the water you promised him." Mila thanked her. They could use it to get DNA to confirm Pastor Burns is Rose's father.

Twenty

"When can I see my dad?" Julian leaned forward anxiously when Mila stepped back into the room, his eyes bloodshot, his face drawn.

Mila threw her leather binder down so it made a loud slapping sound, sat on the edge of the table, crossed her arms and glared down at Julian. "Maybe in twenty-five, thirty years."

Alarm registered in his dark eyes. "Why? Where's my dad?"

"I'm going to be honest with you, Julian. It's not looking good for either of you." She paused and let that statement sink in. "I'm going to give you one chance to tell me the truth about the night Cara was killed. One." She leaned close enough to smell the fear-sweat emanating from his pores and narrowed her eyes. "So what really happened that night?"

Julian's hands began to tremble, his mouth opened and closed as he stared at her. "I.. I don't know."

Mila sighed and moved to the chair across from him. Change of tactics. Her voice softened. "Listen, I get it. You would do anything to keep your family together, to protect your dad. I admire that, I really do. And I can understand why you'd help him in this situation. Why you didn't have a choice."

Julian stared at her, working something out in his head and then his expression changed. Hardened. He shut down. He no longer looked like a scared kid, but like a man pushed to the edge, mentally holding up his fists, ready to fight for his life. And probably his dad's, too. *Shit. She had to break that protective bond he had with Pastor Burns. Was that even possible?*

Mila pulled Cara's printed journal entry from her binder and slid it across the table. "I don't know what your dad told you about the night Cara got pregnant. Maybe you think she was just some slut that seduced your dad." She jabbed a finger at the paper. "But here's the truth. Read it."

His expression shifted again as he glanced from Mila to the paper. His mouth twisted like he tasted something vile. He leaned forward and read. When he was finished, there was a new emotion smoldering in his eyes. Kind of looked like hatred. He pushed the paper back toward her. "Lies."

Mila found herself surprised by his reaction. But then again, he was still protecting his father. "Think about it, Julian. Why would she lie about something in her personal journal, that was password protected by the way, so no one but her would ever see it?"

He threw his hands up. "How should I know? She was probably crazy."

Mila's mouth turned up in a slow smile. *Crazy. Why did they always go there? It was so easy. Don't listen to that woman, she's crazy.* "You know what's crazy, Julian? That living in the home of a pastor hasn't taught you right from wrong. That your moral code is so flexible, you can read a personal account of a girl telling her story about being raped and choose to believe she's lying."

His eyes flicked around the room, his hands slammed on the table, face dark with anger. "Nowhere in there did she say she was raped. How was he supposed to know she wasn't enjoying it? She never said no or told him to stop."

Says every rapist ever. "Are you sexually active, Julian?"

His face reddened and he sat back abruptly. "That's none of your business."

She mirrored him sitting back in the chair. "Okay, you're right. Let me give you some advice either way. If a girl is laying there frozen, not touching you, not engaging, not doing anything but enduring it, she is saying no. She is saying stop." She couldn't shake the image of Cara lying there, her body in freeze mode, unable to fight but just endure the moment. Mila's insides were shaking. There was an unhealed wound bubbling up like a volcano. "I'm going to give you a minute to think about that." She left the room, clicked the door shut and leaned her back against it. Her hand resting on her stomach, she closed her eyes and took in a deep breath, filling her lungs and blowing it out slowly. *Better.*

"You okay?" Frank had walked around the corner and handed her a bottle of water. He must've been done manning the phones and had watched the exchange in the bullpen.

She accepted it, the ice-cold bottle in her palm grounding her. "Thanks. Yeah, just needed a sec."

Frank took a sip from his own bottle and then grinned, showing his pearly veneers. "So you didn't smack the kid?"

She snorted, feeling the tension leave her shoulders. "Something like that."

"I got an old phone book if you need it." His tone was joking but his eyes were appraising her seriously.

"You're showing your age." She rested a hand on his forearm. It was a rare moment of camaraderie and support from him, and she appreciated it. "Thanks, really, I'm okay."

He nodded. "All right. I'm here if you want to tag out. Meanwhile, I'm going to have a talk with Mrs. Pastor. See what she knows."

"Cheers to that." She tapped his water bottle with hers. "No leads on the hotline?"

"Nothing really promising, no. Unless you count the handful of calls about a UFO sighting that night."

Mila groaned. "At this point, aliens would be a relief."

When Mila returned to the interview room, Julian had his elbows resting on his thighs, his brown, wavy hair hanging between his knees. When he lifted his head something in his eyes had changed. The anger had morphed into something different but just as powerful, something painful like grief. He wiped his forearm across his nose, sniffing.

Mila sat silently and watched him.

His body was still, except for one sneakered, shaking foot when he asked, "You said 'the night Cara got pregnant'." He paused and then pulled back his shoulders, made eye contact. He was ready for the truth. "Are you saying that baby... that baby Rose is my father's?"

Mila's mind reeled. She forced her expression to stay neutral. *Did he really not know? What other reason would he have to kill Cara? And if he didn't kill her, how did his hair get on her body that night?* This wasn't adding up. "Yes."

His bottom lip quivered. He bit into it with his top teeth, scraping it hard. "Did he know? That he got Cara pregnant?"

Mila held eye contact. "Yes."

That one word hit him like a blow to the chest, expelling the breath he'd been holding. "Did my mom know?" he asked, looking like he really didn't want to know the answer to this particular question.

"I don't know," Mila said honestly.

A touch of relief surfaced in his eyes, sunk his shoulders. "I don't think she did. It would've really fu... made her sad. She always talked about wanting a baby and stuff. " His head dropped again. More sniffing. More wiping.

She pulled some tissue from the box on the table and handed it to him. "So you haven't seen your mom sad? Or your parents fighting?"

His head swung back and forth like a heavy pendulum. "Nope."

Mila sighed and glanced at the camera. There would be no confession from this kid. She wasn't even sure he had anything to confess. His demeanor was all wrong. Except for that hair. It proved he *was* there. Unless the DNA doesn't match. They wouldn't know that for a while, though.

She was suddenly drained. "All right, come on. I'll take you back to the conference room."

She sat with him until Frank brought Lynnie back in. Her eyes were red and swollen and she stumbled into the room like she was in a daze.

Mila glanced at Frank, and he shook his head. *She didn't know about Rose.*

They watched as Julian stood and took Lynnie in his arms. He was at least a foot taller than her. Her quiet sobs were muffled by his chest. Mila had a twinge of empathy for this close-knit family. At least whichever family members didn't turn out to be murderers.

She and Frank left them alone and went back to the bullpen. They joined Matt and Captain Bartol, forming a semi-circle around the monitor.

The captain had to raise her voice over the noise of the storm pounding the building. Her voice sounded gravelly like it did when she was tired or had to be on the phone all day. "Well, that was a productive morning. At least we got some big questions answered."

"Yep. Why Cara moved to Edgewater and where the money came from," Mila stated.

"What's our next move?" Frank asked.

I'm going to release them," Captain Bartol said with a sigh. "We don't have enough for an arrest warrant, and it's getting too dangerous to travel out there."

"Boy would I love to be a fly on the wall during that car ride home," Matt said.

"They'll have a lot to talk about for sure." Captain Bartol glanced at Frank. "Why don't you go ahead and tell them they can go home. Then work on a search warrant for their house so we can get that done as soon as the storm passes. We need to prove one of them had access to benzos."

Frank pushed himself out of the chair. "It'd also be great if they were dumb enough to keep the receipt for the wine."

A gruff laugh came from the captain as she stood and stretched out her knee. "Sure or hid some bloody clothes in the hamper. We should be so lucky." After Frank left, she turned to Matt. "All right, Matt, your work is done. You can get out of here."

He nodded gratefully. He didn't have a family, but he had two rescued chihuahuas that were like his kids. "See you all on the other side of Henry."

"Be careful driving home." She addressed Mila. "Heard anything back from Aiden yet?"

"No." She glanced at her Fitbit. Four-thirty. "He should be back soon."

Another hour passed before Aiden appeared in the doorway of the conference room where Captain Bartol and Mila were having vending machine crackers and fresh coffee for dinner and listening to the storm rage outside. Mila had also had a warm, canned protein shake, which was threatening to upset her stomach.

Aiden's curls were dark with rain that dripped down his face. He reached for some napkins on the table and tried to dry himself off.

"How'd it go?" Mila asked.

He made a disapproving face at her cracker dinner as he dropped in the chair across from her. "Roads are getting flooded. Sustained winds have almost reached the point where patrol will start heading in." The energy he brought was high, worried. They were almost out of time. He took a seat and pulled out his notebook. "The house is a rental with two twenty-one-year-old roommates living there. They both acknowledged seeing Julian at the party Friday night, but neither one could say if he left at any point. I did call the girl, Shelly Nowak, and she said she saw Julian arrive at the party around 9:30 pm and they hung out for about an hour. Then she didn't see him again after that. She looked for him around midnight since they'd agreed to share the cost of an Uber home, but couldn't find him." He paused and really looked at Mila then Captain Bartol. His eyes narrowed. "Okay, what did I miss?"

The captain rose from her chair with a tired grunt. "So much. But I'll let Mila fill you in. Sounds like it's time to help get the media room ready for the troops."

Aiden sat in stunned silence when Mila finished telling him about the journal, the night Cara got pregnant and Pastor Burns's version of what happened. He glanced at the board, where some of the answers had been added to the questions. "Do you think they were in on it together? The Pastor and Julian?"

"Maybe. Pastor Burns had the motive, Julian had the hair found on the body. Maybe along with Lynnie. I'd say she had motive, also. Plus it's the only way the pastor's alibi doesn't check out. If she is covering for him." Mila's phone buzzed. She didn't recognize the number. "Detective Harlow."

"Mila?" It was Charlie. "Something strange just happened and I don't know if I'm being paranoid or…" Rose was fussing in the background.

"Better paranoid than not right now. What happened?" Aiden's attention cut sharply to her.

"Well, I went into the nursery to change Rose and could see through the blinds. The hurricane shutter had fallen off. I mean, the window is locked, so we're safe. But, that's weird, right?"

Mila's chest tightened. Hurricane shutters don't just fall off. They are fastened by heavy bolts and wing nuts to the exterior of the house. An image of the shoe print below Rose's window on the night of Cara's murder flashed in her mind. Were they right? Had the killer come to the house to take Rose? "Make sure all the windows and doors are locked. I'll be right there."

"What's going on?" Aiden asked as he watched Mila scramble out of the chair.

"Someone removed the hurricane shutter from Rose's bedroom window. Tell the captain I'm going over there to check it out. I'll stay with Charlie and Rose during the storm if I have to."

"Let me know when you get there. And avoid Grove St. It's probably impassable by now."

"Probably lots of roads impassable by now," she whispered, the urgency stealing her breath. "I'll get there somehow."

"Hey." Adien stood and touched her arm before she ran out. "What time did the Captain let the Burns family go home?"

Mila glanced up at the clock on the wall. "About an hour and a half ago." It dawned on her why he was asking, and her heart rate ticked up a notch.

Aiden saw her understanding. "Yeah, so be careful. You guys have poked the bear. If Pastor Burns or his son feel threatened, they are going to get desperate. Desperate people do stupid things."

She nodded. "I'll keep you updated as long as I can."

Twenty-one

After a white-knuckle drive, with visibility being zilch even with wipers on high, Mila pulled into the driveway. Luckily it sloped upward enough that it wasn't flooded yet. The roads were a different story. More than once, she'd had to floor it to get through accumulated water that was halfway up her tires, sending wide arcs of spray over the roof. Fortunately, she'd only come across one other truck trying to navigate through the torrential rains and winds. She hoped he'd made it to wherever he was trying to go. The world was completely gray now, branches and debris floating down the streets, flying through the air, palm trees whipping back and forth. Just stepping out of the SUV would be an act of faith.

She tightened the drawstrings around her rain hood and pushed against the car door. A heavy gust pushed back, slamming the door shut. She pushed again, this time the wind ripping it out of her hand and throwing it open. She slid out. The assault of cold pounding rain on her face took her breath away. Hunching over to protect her face, she raced around to the side of the house, splashing through water up to her ankles, fighting the push and pull of the sustained winds. There it was. The shutter lay next to the house. Not a natural position if it had fallen off.

Crouching low, she searched desperately around in the flooded mulch, below the window until her fingers brushed two of the wingnuts. The pounding rain was assaulting her back, so two would have to do. Wrestling the rectangular piece of aluminum back in place over the window, she threw her body against it and held it in place. Something smacked into the back of her calf and she winced. Ignoring the pain, she twisted one wingnut back in place in the upper left-hand corner and then the lower right-hand corner. Better than nothing. At least if it stayed, it would keep flying debris from breaking the window.

Hugging the house's outer wall and crouching low against the wind, she made her way back around to the front door.

Before she could knock, Charlie had the door opened and was pulling her in. "You okay?" Charlie was holding Rose and they were both staring at her wide-eyed like she'd just arrived from another planet.

Mila undid the drawstring and pushed the hoodie off. A lot of good it did, her hair was still dripping down her face. "Fine. Got the shutter back up. Hope it holds." She slipped her water-logged shoes and socks off.

"Let me get you a towel." Charlie and Rose disappeared down the hall. When she returned she said, "here's a pair of Cara's sweatpants. We can throw yours in the dryer."

"Thank you." Mila had peeled off her raincoat and also left that by the front door. She accepted the sweatpants and began rubbing the towel over her head and arms. "Anything else happen?"

"No, nothing. Maybe I overreacted." She was chewing on her thumbnail. Rose was pulling at her own shirt, beginning to fuss again. "The storm's just making me a bit jumpy."

Mila decided not to tell her she wasn't overreacting. Someone had removed that shutter and the only reason someone would do that would be to get to Rose. "It's fine. I was in the neighborhood."

Charlie laughed and readjusted Rose in her arms. "All right, you can change in the bathroom. The dryer's behind the accordion door in the hallway. Can I get you something to drink? I have water, iced tea and wine."

"Iced tea sounds great." She was still on duty, though Charlie didn't have to know that, either. After she changed into the sweatpants, she opened the cabinet above the dryer and placed her duty belt and Glock on the top shelf. She'd retrieve it with her dried pants. Before she shut the cabinet door, she thought about unloading the gun for safety. Then again, someone had removed that hurricane shutter on Rose's bedroom window. The threat was still out there. Either Pastor Burns or Julian could be that threat as they'd been released from the station. No, she'd leave it loaded. Besides Rose couldn't reach it and Charlie was no threat.

Then she texted Aiden that she'd made it to the house. She walked over, picked up a stuffed frog from the floor and handed it to Rose, who was now fussing in a small playpen while Charlie was in the kitchen. "Hey, brave girl. How you holding up?" Rose waved her arms excitedly and then grasped the frog, pulling it directly to her mouth. "She's teething?" Mila called behind her.

Charlie appeared and handed her a glass of iced tea. "Yeah, I think. I honestly don't know much about babies. I hope I don't completely screw her up."

Mila smiled to herself, remembering saying those exact words to Paul. "It's harder to do than you think."

Mila took a long drink, surprised at how thirsty she was, considering she'd almost been drowned in the downpour. She set the glass on the end table and took a seat on the sofa, briefly glancing at the muted TV, where the weather girl was standing in front of the image of Henry, the blue and fluorescent green bands rotating, overlapping the edge of their coast. The angry red eye was still offshore. Looks like landfall had shifted a little more north again, but they were still getting the outer bands. Winds were up to 105 mph. Stronger than they expected. She checked her calve where it was pulsating. A shadow of a bruise and swelling. No cut, so no risk of infection.

Charlie sat beside her and angled her body so she could watch Rose.

Mila decided to just rip off the Band-Aid. "We found out some information tonight. About Rose." She held Charlie's gaze as she said, "Rose was conceived when Cara was raped by a pastor at the church where she went for help, because she was afraid her boyfriend was going to kill her."

"What?" The word was carried from Charlie's lips on a breathy exhale. Her gaze flicked to Rose. "Oh my God."

"And that's why your sister came to Edgewater. The pastor, Pastor Burns, now works here. He gave her the money to move here. He wanted to see Rose grow up, just not be part of her life... as a father."

Tears were rolling from Charlie's eyes. She didn't bother to wipe them away. "Did he kill her? Did he kill Cara?"

"That we don't know yet."

Charlie was shaking her head. She pinched her eyes shut. "Oh, Cara. Why didn't you tell me?" A heart-breaking sob escaped her. She opened her eyes, they were so full of pain and pleading, Mila felt her own heart contract. "Why didn't she come to me? I could've helped her."

Mila reached over and squeezed her hand. "I don't know, but it was her decision. You can't take on the guilt of someone else's life decisions. Even people you love."

They sat in silence for a while, watching Rose babble to herself, playing with the toys scattered around the playpen. Mila tuned out the howling winds rattling the shutters and went back over the case in her mind, rehashing everything they'd learned from the Burns family today. The only two who seemed innocent were the wheelchair-bound grandfather and Jorge.

"Oh, oh no." Charlie said, interrupting Mila's train of thought. She was leaning forward, her attention on the ceiling in the corner.

Mila followed her gaze. A large bubble had formed under the paint and was beginning to drip from the center. "I'll grab a pot." She went to the kitchen, rummaged around beneath the cabinets until she found a large soup pot. As she placed it on the floor beneath the leak, a text came through.

It was from Aiden. They'd received an answer back from SICAR—Shoeprint Image Capture and Retrieval—a database used to identify sole patterns of shoeprints left at crime scenes.

They are identified as Converse Chucks, size unknown, wear undetermined. Note: not the shoes Cara was wearing when killed. Checked recordings. Julian wearing Converse. Frank added them to search warrant.

"Everything okay?" Charlie asked.

Mila pulled her gaze from her phone. "Yeah. Just my colleague checking in."

She wandered back over to the sofa. Even with the hair sample match, she'd been questioning how much Julian was involved. Mainly because of his reaction... he really seemed like he hadn't known Pastor Burns was Rose's father. So what would be his motive to kill Cara? Just because the pastor told him to? Maybe if both his parents convinced him he had to do it to protect the family.

She still felt like she was missing something.

Maybe Pastor Burns didn't send him there to kill Cara, just drug her with the benzos in the wine. That would make sense since whoever killed her hadn't brought their own weapon. Why drug her? The only reason that made sense was to get Cara out of the way so they could grab Rose. But surely, they didn't think they could get away with kidnapping a baby? Then again, the pastor said he didn't know Cara had a sister. Maybe they thought there would be no one for Cara to turn to.

She rubbed the spot above her eye that was starting to ache and stared at Rose. The little girl had pulled herself up in the playpen and was reaching for Charlie. Charlie lifted her up and hugged her to her chest. "Maybe she's hungry." She carried her into the kitchen, talking softly to her.

Mila spotted another leak in the ceiling. She followed Charlie to the kitchen and pulled out another pot from the cabinet. "Old Mr. Tally is not going to be happy about this."

"I'll be happy as long as the roof holds," Charlie said nervously as the power flickered.

As Charlie fed Rose oatmeal and Mila inspected the ceiling for any more leaks, there was a pounding on the door. The two women glanced at each other, startled.

"Who in the world would be out in this?" Charlie asked.

Mila held up a hand to stop her from going to the door. Then she sprang down the hall and retrieved her Glock from the shelf. The pounding came again. There was no peephole, so Mila held her weapon against her leg, pressed herself against the wall and opened the door. A flash of lightning blinded her for a split second as thunder boomed and rain blew sideways into the house.

Twenty-two

A figure stumbled into the living room, draped in an oversized yellow raincoat. A deep sob came from beneath the hood. Mila forced the door shut, battling the wind. The figure whirled around, her eyes registering the gun and held up her hands. "It's me." She pushed off the hood. "Jemma."

"Jesus, Jemma." Mila pointed the Glock at the floor, her heart still hammering. "What are you doing out in the storm?"

Her eyelids were swollen, nose red from crying. "I just needed to see Rose. Is it true?" She glanced behind her at the baby then back to Mila. "Is it true Dad raped Cara? That Rose is his?"

She could just imagine the devastating conversation the family had with her when they got home. "Yes, I'm afraid so."

Jemma stumbled over to the kitchen and slipped her finger into Rose's grip. The baby blew a raspberry, sending oatmeal all over the highchair. "I have a baby sister." Jemma smiled and looked up at Charlie, eyes glassy and wide. "I babysat all the time for Cara."

Charlie wiped the oatmeal off Rose's chin with a dishtowel. "Oh, good. I can pick your brain about things Rose does and doesn't like." She noticed the puddle of water forming around Jemma's feet. "Why don't you take off that coat and go grab a towel. There's no way you're going back out until this storm passes."

Mila returned her weapon to the shelf above the dryer and settled back down to watch Henry on the TV as he slowly stalked them. Jemma had dropped her wet items by the front door and was wrapping a beach towel she'd grabbed from the bathroom around her shoulders. She took a seat in the chair cattycorner to Mila.

"So, how did you get here?" Mila asked. "You drove?"

Jemma rubbed her hair with the towel. "More like floated here. A boat would've been more helpful." Jemma's face took on a shadow of determination then anger. "I know it was stupid and dangerous. But Julian told me what happened at the police station. Mom won't come out of her room. She's devastated. We heard her scream that she wants a divorce. So what's going to happen to us? To me and Julian? Our family is all broken now."

Charlie shot Mila a meaningful look then picked up Rose. "I'm just going to go wash her off and get her a new diaper. Be back."

Jemma watched them disappear down the hall. "I can see it now. Rose's resemblance to Dad."

Mila heard the quiet anger behind her words. "People have worked through worse things. I wouldn't give up on your family yet. Besides you and Julian won't be going back in the system. Even if you two have to split your time between two homes, you still have both your parents." Unless the pastor and his wife were involved in Cara's death. Then they'd be in prison. "And you will always have each other."

Jemma pulled the towel tighter around her as a peal of thunder added to the chaotic sounds of the hurricane assaulting the house. "I wish we had San… I mean Jorge, too. He always had my back."

Mila stayed silent. That was out of her hands.

Charlie returned without Rose. "She seemed sleepy, so I put her in her crib. We'll see if she actually falls asleep."

"Sounds like you're getting to know her," Mila said.

Charlie plopped down on the couch with a tired smile. "A little. She really is such a happy baby most of the time. Though once in a while she'll wear herself out crying inconsolably. I think she misses her mom." She rubbed her eyes then turned to Jemma. "So, what can you tell me about Rose? Don't leave anything out."

Jemma talked for a good half hour about all the things she knew about Rose, her likes and dislikes, the food and nap routine Cara tried to keep her on. "Her favorite food is sweet potatoes, and she loves baths and loves when you sing to her."

At one point, Jemma went to the bathroom. After she'd been in there awhile, Mila went to check on her and heard crying. She knocked on the door and asked if she was okay. Jemma insisted she was fine, just sad about her family. Understandable and nothing Mila could say to console her.

Rose had ended up falling asleep, so Charlie made a frozen pizza. They ate and watched the Weather Channel's coverage of Henry while they still had power. Mila was surprised it had held out this long. Luckily, the storm had a relatively small radius, so they only had about an hour left before the eye would pass just north of them and the wind direction would change. Currently the wind gusts recorded in their area were reaching 120 mph, with sustained winds of 90 mph. The shutters were rattling against the house, the rain pounding on the roof, the wind against the house ranging from whispers to roars. They also had to place more pots on the floor to catch leaks from the ceiling.

"Why do the newscasters put themselves at risk like that?" Mila shook her head as the news moved to a live feed of a reporter standing out in the storm in Tampa Bay, battling to hold his ground against the winds as he shouted through the heavy rain. Boats rocked in the frenzied waves of the Bay behind him. A large palm frond flew between him and the cameraman.

"I ask my husband that," Charlie said. "He's a movie director. He said entertainment's not for wimps."

"Neither are hurricanes," Mila said. She wasn't fond of hurricanes, but patience was one of her strong suits, so waiting it out didn't make her anxious. What did was the noise, the ceaseless hours and hours of unrelenting noise. It was like living through a banshee howling contest. Air Pods would've been helpful. "Speaking of your husband, is he okay with being an instant dad?"

Charlie's expression softened. "We'd actually been talking about having a baby. He came from a big family so he's totally on board." She pulled her feet up beneath her and hugged her knees. "Though I'm not sure I'm prepared, honestly. Just from these past few days, I can see how raising a baby is an all-consuming job. I'm working sixty-hour weeks, corporate law, as it is. Balancing that isn't going to be easy. Do you have kids?"

Mila smiled. "A daughter, Harper. She's ten."

"You have a demanding job. How do you do it?"

"There really is no such thing as balance. But, I'm lucky... I have a mother-in-law who lives with us and helps out with Harper."

Charlie pursed her lips in thought. "I guess a full-time nanny is an option."

They talked about raising kids for a while longer and then Mila excused herself to check her texts, answered ones from Paul and her dad and brothers letting them know she was fine. She was actually surprised to see the one from her older brother, Dean. They had never really been close, and he had moved to New York after college to work in finance. They didn't have anything in common, but she did appreciate him checking on her. She closed the bathroom door and video-called Kittie.

"How's it going?" Mila asked.

"Good. Good. We're all hunkered down. You at the station?"

"No. I'm actually at our vic's house with her baby and sister. It's all shuttered up though, we should be fine." The lights flickered as if in warning, but they miraculously stayed on. "How's Harper? She seemed nervous when I talked to her last."

Kitty's gaze flicked to her right, where Harper must be. "We still have power here at Paul's, so she's fine for now. I'm keeping her busy. We're practicing knitting. Let me put her on."

Harper's face filled the screen, her smile dimpling her round cheeks and her blue eyes shining. Mila's anxiety ticked down a few notches. "Hi, Mom. Look what I'm making." Harper turned the phone to show her mom a wonky blue and white square of knit yarn then back to herself. "It's going to be a blanket for Iggy. Maybe he'll stop stealing my socks."

Mila studied her daughter's face, looking for any sign Harper was anxious about the storm. Kittie seemed to be doing a good job distracting her. "That's great, sweetie, better than I could do. How are the dogs and Iggy?"

Harper rolled her eyes. "Max is with Dad at the station. Dad put the baby pool with cat litter in the garage for Oscar to potty, but he won't use it. He just whines at the door."

Of course, Paul was at the station. "Well, if he has to go bad enough, he'll use it."

"That's what Dad said when I texted him." The phone shook as Harper held it at arm's length so Mila could see Iggy resting on her shoulder. "Guess what I found out Iggy likes?" She didn't wait for Mila to guess. "Watermelon."

"Better than peanut M&M's." Mila smiled at her daughter, but a pang of guilt hit her. She should be there with Harper. What kind of mom was she? Time to go before the guilt distracted her from her job. "Okay, I'll call you again when I can. Love you to the moon and back."

When she returned, Charlie had brought out a Scrabble game she found in Cara's boxes. The three of them played, chatted and kept an eye on the TV for updates until the electricity flickered again and then went out. They moaned in unison. It was about to get hot and stuffy without the AC.

Charlie went around and turned on the battery-powered lanterns she'd strategically placed around the house. They created weird shadows on the walls. Without the noise of the TV and the air conditioning blowing, the storm's rage seemed louder, more menacing in the silence. Mila thought about sleepovers when she was younger, giggling girls with flashlights in a dark bedroom telling spooky stories. Haunted houses, scary movies. Humans just loved to be scared. As long as the threat wasn't real.

Unfortunately for them, it was very real.

Twenty-three

Mila noticed water seeping in under the front door. She went to the hall closet and grabbed a handful of towels. Pressing them against the bottom of the door, she then worked to sop up the leak with another towel. She moved Jemma's yellow raincoat to wipe the floor and froze. Beneath it were her wet socks and shoes. Black Converse.

She glanced behind her. Unfortunately, Jemma was looking right at her. Mila shot her what she hoped was a reassuring smile then covered them up with the coat and stood slowly. Holding the wet towel, she tried to decide if this meant anything. After all, they knew Julian also had Converse. Jemma didn't even know about Rose until tonight. Or did she? Could she be that good of an actress?

Mila went back to sit on the couch, eyeing Jemma as the teen tapped on her phone, softly at first and then harder.

Jemma groaned. "I can't get a signal." She glanced up at Mila. "What network do you have? Do you have service?"

Mila pulled out her phone. No bars. She tried to send a text and got the spinny wheel then a red exclamation point. *Crap.* She dialed Aiden's number and got the 'this call cannot be completed at this time' response. "I don't have service, either." This was the part of hurricanes that made her nervous. Cut off from her backup, cut off from her daughter. She needed to know if she could trust Jemma. "You know, I was thinking. You're very lucky to have such a close relationship with Julian. He told us he took the blame for the front-end damage to the car. But it was actually you who was driving when it happened."

Jemma's head jerked up from her phone. Was that suspicion narrowing her eyes? "He told you that?"

Mila nodded, waiting to see if she would deny it.

Instead, her mood visibly shifted, darkened. She clenched her phone in her lap. "Yeah. The boys were always protective of me. I just can't believe Jorge won't be with us anymore."

"Do you think Julian will be protective of Rose, too? Now that he knows?" Mila was trying to remind her she still had Julian.

"Maybe." She threw her phone on the cushion beside her, shoved her fingers in her hair, clutched it at the scalp and rested her elbows on her knees.

A memory flashed of Julian doing the same thing at the station when he got upset. *The hair.* A prickling sensation crawled up Mila's spine.

Could it have been Jemma's hair and not Julian's? After all, microscopic comparison is more of an art than an exact science, and it can't say with certainty who the hair came from without a DNA analysis. They both had the same color, texture and wave.

Mila rubbed the tightening space between her brows with her thumb.

Was she just trying to force pieces of the puzzle together that didn't belong?

She thought back to the first time she met Jemma, sitting on the altar at their church, absolutely devastated. She was definitely upset about Cara's death. No faking that. *And what would be her motive to kill Cara?* Same as Julian's... keep Rose a secret so the scandal didn't destroy their family. They had been through so much in group and foster homes, even being separated from each other. What wouldn't they do to keep their family together? But while Julian barely knew

Cara, Jemma considered her a friend. *Was she capable of such brutality against someone she cared about?*

Rose should be safe now, though. Now that the cat's out of the bag, everyone in the family knows, including Lynnie. So, why would someone remove the hurricane shutter on Rose's window if they weren't trying to take her? Maybe it hadn't been attached right and did blow off? She shifted on the sofa in irritation. It was so hard to think with the constant deafening barrage against the house.

Charlie had been listening to their conversation quietly. "Jemma, I can send you photos of Rose and bring her back to visit once in a while if you'd like?"

Jemma slowly shifted her attention to Charlie. She stared at her for a long moment, seemingly lost in thought. Then a quiet, "sure."

Charlie shot Mila a worried look.

Mila decided she needed to fill Charlie in on what she'd been thinking so she didn't make Jemma any more promises about Rose. She stood. "Hey, Charlie, can you show me the book you were talking about in Cara's bedroom?"

Charlie blinked and then seemed to understand. She smiled tightly. "Oh, the book... okay." She grabbed a lantern and led the way down the squat hall.

Mila clicked the bedroom door shut behind them. It was already getting stuffy and stale in the small room without air conditioning.

Charlie put the lantern on the dresser and crossed her arms. "What's up?" she whispered.

The room was dark in the corners where the lantern light didn't reach. Something large thudded against the roof. They glanced up in unison. The roof held. Mila moved closer to Charlie. "There are a few things that are making me wonder if Jemma was involved in your sister's death."

Charlie's eyes widened, shadows from the lantern creating dark hallows beneath them. "Like what?" she whispered harshly.

Mila hesitated but then decided if it was her sister, she would want to know. "The shoe print beneath Rose's bedroom window came back as a match for Converse, which both Julian and Jemma wear. Also, the physical characteristics of the hair found on Cara's body seem to be a match for Julian, though he and Jemma share those characteristics as well. The hair will be sent for DNA analysis to be sure, but that takes time. I think we just need to be cautious with Jemma right now."

"Oh." Charlie's mouth twisted. "That doesn't seem like very much. A shoe and a hair? I mean, Jemma just doesn't strike me as a killer. She's so sweet with Rose." She was struggling, obviously not wanting to believe the teen they'd been getting to know the last few hours was capable of murder.

Unfortunately, everyone was capable of violence given the right circumstances. But were these the right circumstances for Jemma? That's what Mila had to find out.

A soft cry came from behind the door.

"Rose is up." Charlie plucked the lantern from the dresser. "Probably getting too hot to sleep in there."

A louder wail broke through the howling, whistling winds.

Mila grabbed Charlie's arm and held a finger up to her lips. She cocked her head toward the door. The cries were muffled, further away than they should be. Mila's hand went to her waist. *Shit.* Her weapon was still on the shelf in the laundry closet.

"What's wrong?" Charlie's words were breathless with fear.

"Just stay behind me," Mila commanded. She moved to the door and opened it slowly. Rose's fussy cries were louder but were definitely not coming from her bedroom.

Charlie's whisper was right behind Mila. "Jemma probably got Rose when she heard her wake up."

That was one possibility. The other was she was on the right track about Jemma and Rose was in danger. She couldn't take that chance.

"Turn off the lantern," Mila commanded. "And stay here." She crept into the hallway. Rose's protests were now more fussy than crying. Maybe Jemma had got Rose when she heard her wake up and was consoling her. The tightness in Mila's gut was a warning that she never ignored, though. She reached up above the shelf and grabbed her duty belt. Her blood ran cold. The Glock was gone. *Stupid, Mila.* Jemma had gone to the bathroom while she was putting it back there. She must've been watching.

Placing the belt back on the shelf, she pressed her back against the wall, scooted forward and peered into the dim living room.

Jemma had slipped into her raincoat and shoes. She had Rose against her chest, zipped up inside, just her brown curls peeking out. Mila's weapon was on the table by the door.

Mila stepped out into the open, palms out. "Jemma, this is a really bad idea. It's too dangerous out there."

Jemma's head whipped up and she swiped the Glock off the table, pointed it at Mila. "I know you guys were talking about me. Don't try to stop us. I can't let Rose go live in Miami away from us. Now that Mom knows, Rose belongs with us. She can fix our family."

There was a cry behind Mila, and she felt a rush of air brush past her. *Charlie.* Mila tried to grab for her arm, but it was too late.

"No, please!" Charlie cried, stumbling into the living room, her attention locked on Rose. "Please don't take her out there. You'll both be killed. We can work something—"

A loud bang. Charlie's scream. Rose's piercing cry. It all happened in slow motion as Mila moved to Charlie, who had fallen to the floor, blood pooling beneath her.

Jemma howled, "Forgive me," the same words carved on Cara's thighs. The door opened, the winds and rain now roaring inside the house.

"Rose!" Charlie sobbed, her face contorted in pain.

"It'll be okay. Deep breaths." Mila's heart was beating so hard, she could hear it in her ears, drowning out the roar of the winds. If the bullet hit anything major, they were screwed. No ambulance, no way to get her to the hospital safely. She grabbed a beach towel off the couch, lifted Charlie's T-shirt and pressed it against the wound. When the blood seeped into the towel, she raised it and examined the wound. She let out the breath she'd been holding. "She just nicked your side. You're going to be okay."

Charlie was crying so hard, her face was beet red and she was beginning to hyperventilate.

"I need you to take in a long, deep breath." Mila demonstrated, trying to get her to follow, but Charlie's eyes were wild and panicked. "Look at me!" Mila instructed. When Charlie got her eyes to focus, Mila once again demonstrated deep, slow breaths.

After Charlie's chest was no longer heaving and her eyes were finally focused on Mila, she nodded. Before Mila could do anything else, she had to shut the front door. There was already an inch of water on the floor. She forced it shut, unable to see anything in the darkness outside and then slipped as she hurried back to Charlie. Just from those few seconds, she was soaked. "Okay, I'm going to stop this bleeding and then go after Rose. Think you can stand?"

Charlie squeezed her eyes shut, sending fresh tears streaming down her cheeks into her ears. She nodded.

"Slowly," Mila said, helping her sit up.

Charlie cried out but let Mila pull her to her feet. "Easy." Mila walked her to the couch where she helped her lie, putting a pillow under her head. Then she hurried to the bathroom, where she'd seen a first aid kit under the sink. She grabbed it, a bottle of Ibuprofen and wet a washcloth under the faucet.

"Please find Rose," Charlie was whispering over and over, almost delirious. "Cara will never forgive me."

"I'll find her. As soon as we get this bleeding under control." Mila wiped off the fresh blood on Charlie's side then opened the First Aid kit. She chose a large cotton pad and a spool of gauze. Charlie winced as Mila pressed it against the wound and wrapped the gauze tight around her stomach. "All right. That should do until we can get you to the hospital." She poured a glass of water from the kitchen and helped Charlie swallow two Ibuprofen. With labored breath and her thoughts on Rose, Mila glanced around, spotted Charlie's phone. She placed it beside her. "In case the network comes back up." She grabbed her hand. "Hey, I'm going to do everything I can to bring Rose back to you. I promise."

Charlie forced a smile. Her face was paler than normal and beaded with sweat. "I know you will."

Mila's stomach tightened. *Had she just made a promise she couldn't keep?*

Twenty-four

Mila dressed back in her pants and duty belt, which felt too empty and light without her Glock. Then she slipped into her rain jacket, which would be just about useless in a hurricane. With one glance back at a distraught Charlie crying on the sofa, she opened the door and began the push against the wind, sheets of rain and water past her ankles to her SUV.

With quick reflexes, she dodged a strip of siding that came tumbling out of the darkness toward her, propelled by the hundred-mile-an-hour winds. When she was safely inside the rocking SUV, engine on and wipers going, she took a second to think.

Where would Jemma take Rose? Back to her home? Probably not, because that's the first place Mila would look. *Would Jemma harm Rose?* If she was cornered, maybe. But Mila didn't think she'd want to. Her motive seemed to be to keep Rose here with her family. Obviously still in denial or delusional. Mila would have to be careful with her fragile emotional state.

And then she thought about the fact that people return to the scene of the crime and wondered… would she go back to the beach? She had to check because that would be the most dangerous place for them right now, out in the elements. If Jemma had taken Rose back to her house, they'd be safe there for now. She had to at least make sure they weren't at the beach.

What should've been a five-minute drive in normal conditions turned into twenty as Mila maneuvered her vehicle down dark roads like rushing rivers. It was almost ten-thirty at night and a grayed-out nightmare. Rain didn't just fall, it crashed like buckets of water thrown at her windshield making her reflexively tap her brakes. The only things visible were the tops of palm trees whipping back and forth, up and down in supplication, bending to Henry's will. Her heart raced. Her fingers were aching from clutching the steering wheel so tight. Palm fronds and other debris kept hitting her SUV, and at one point, a vicious gust blew her off the road.

"Come on, Come on," she growled, as she shoved the gear shift in reverse, hit the gas then put it into drive, mashing the gas pedal over and over. Panic constricted her chest. What if she couldn't get out of this? Minutes counted right now. Tears of frustration prickled her eyes and she shoved the gear back in reverse. No. Getting stuck here was not an option. Her jaw clenched with determination as she continued to battle the saturated yard her tires were sunk into. Reverse. Gas. Forward. Gas. She rocked the SUV back and forth until the last time she gunned it, it lurched onto the road. She gasped with relief.

Leaning forward in the seat, she squinted through the windshield to navigate. Almost there. Once more, the vehicle fishtailed as it got caught on a curb, but Mila got it under control. Peering through the sheets of rain as she made the final turn, her headlights finally swept the beach parking lot. The white Corolla sat abandoned in the parking lot. *No, no, no.* Her heart dropped into her stomach. Not what she wanted to see.

She pulled in next to it, jumped out and, fighting the winds, pulled open the driver's door. Jemma and Rose were gone. But Mila's Glock was sitting on the floorboard of the passenger side. Leaning over, she retrieved it and shoved it back into her holster.

The ocean was angry and loud, with rolling white caps and large waves crashing onshore, sending foam flying in the roaring winds. Mila's flashlight barely made a dent in the darkness. But it kept her oriented so she could stay as close to the dunes as possible for some cover.

She almost lost the flashlight as she got propelled forward and fell more times than she could count. Her palms were raw from hitting the coarse sand hard every time she fell. She crawled a few feet each time, chin tucked to try to get a few panting breaths in before she stood and was hit in the face with the full force of the hurricane once again. Her eyes were stinging, her leg muscles burning, every inch forward a battle. There, in the dark, in the dangerous winds, she had never felt so alone. It was like being on a different planet and she had to force herself not to panic, not to turn around. No, even if it was a slim chance Jemma had brought Rose here, she had to check. Fighting her anxiety, she pushed forward.

What seemed like an eternity later, the lifeguard stand finally appeared like a mirage in a flash of lightning. Relief made her cry out, but the sound was swept from her mouth instantly.

Climbing the stairs put her in a more vulnerable position. She had to keep low and concentrate. But finally, she hit the last two steps and propelled herself inside the wood structure. Breathing hard from the effort, she raised her eyes from beneath her dripping hood and there was Jemma. A mixture of relief and anger washed over her. Jemma was lying on the floor on her stomach, her palm pressed to the dark blood stain engrained in the wood. Where Cara had taken her last breath. *Yeah, she had definitely been here when Cara had died. But had she been alone?*

Mila's gaze swept the small structure. Rose wasn't here. Mila's heart pounded against her chest wall. What had she done with Rose?

They had some protection from the storm in here, but the winds were still roaring outside the wooden walls and the rain was still spraying in through the door. The stand was also rocking, so Mila had to remind herself the structure had withstood stronger hurricanes than this one.

Mila scooted in to sit next to Jemma and rested a hand on her back. "Jemma."

Jemma jumped, her head jerking up, eyes wide as she stared at Mila like she was a ghost. Her eyes were empty, lost. Her nostril had blood beneath it, and she looked like a child.

"Jemma, where's Rose?" Mila tried and failed to keep the urgency out of her tone.

Jemma pushed herself up slowly and wrapped her arms around her knees. "She's safe."

Mila sat in front of Jemma, looking into her fully dilated eyes, trying to decide if she believed her. After all, she had just watched her shoot Charlie and put Rose's life in danger by taking her out into a hurricane. Mila raised her voice above the storm. It was creating a sense of urgency that had her on nerves on edge. "Jemma, I want to believe that. But I need you to tell me the truth. It's time to come clean. Where is Rose?"

Jemma's mouth was slack, she looked dazed. Her eyes moved from Mila to the dark square of nature's fury beyond the doorway.

"Is Charlie okay?" Jemma, too, had to shout above the howling winds. "I'm sorry. I panicked."

Mila scooted closer, less space for their voices to have to carry. There was a loud peal of thunder, a blinding flash of lightning. She had to get Jemma out of here. Had to get the teen to take her to Rose. Mila was out of patience. "Where's Rose, Jemma?" she shouted.

Jemma slowly moved her gaze to hold Mila's. There was something new and dark glistening in her eyes. Mila didn't like it. *Despair? Defeat? Surrender?* "I'll show you."

Jemma pushed herself up, her head disappearing beneath the raincoat hood. Carefully, she made her way down the rickety wooden steps, crawling backward on her hands and knees. Mila was behind her, climbing down the same way in the dark, gripping the edge of the steps so the wind didn't catch her and push her over the side. She could hear nothing but the raging winds in her ears, the angry surf crashing on the shore.

She hoped Jemma was leading her back to the parking lot. Hoped the little girl wasn't out here somewhere. She stopped her mind right there.

When Mila reached the last few missing steps, she slid, letting her feet dangle until she touched solid ground and then dropped. She grunted as her ankle turned beneath her and a heavy gust shoved her backwards. Swearing into the wind, she got back on her hands and knees, braced her feet far apart and pushed herself up to standing. She squinted through the blowing sheets of rain around her. Jemma was gone.

"Jemma!" she screamed. Her voice was instantly swept away. She could only see a few feet in front of her, so Jemma could be close and she wouldn't know it. *Damn it.*

Would she make a run for it? Head to the car and try to get away?

Mila thought about that dark look in Jemma's eyes. *Defeat. Hopelessness.*

No. She wasn't going to make a run for it.

Mila pressed forward, toward the ocean, her jacket whipping violently around her body, her eyes tearing from the winds, her face numb from the stinging cold rain. More than once a heavy gust blew her sideways or forward, sending her tumbling into the wet, hard sand, jarring her body. When she finally reached the shoreline, she screamed Jemma's name again. Again it was swept away, ineffective against nature's roar. She was up to her knees in the rough surf, scanning the surprisingly warm, turbulent waters when a crack of lightning gave her the break she needed.

In the flash of light, she caught a figure about ten feet in front of her, just disappearing beneath a breaking wave. Without hesitation, she dove into the surf, feeling the resistance as it tried to push her back onto shore. She was a strong swimmer though and vanished beneath the next wave and the next, until her head broke the surface where she last saw Jemma.

She turned in the water, head swiveling, eyes scanning the chop through the heavy rain. She coughed as a rogue wave smacked her in the face, and she got a mouthful of saltwater. Undeterred, she kicked her legs, turning and searching with laser focus.

There! Jemma's head surfaced to her right. She dove back in, her arms moving in strong strokes, her legs kicking. Her hand suddenly touched something solid, and she grabbed on. Still holding tight, her head broke through the water. She coughed as the rain tried to drown her. But relief flooded her instead as she saw she was holding Jemma's arm.

That relief was short-lived as she realized Jemma wasn't conscious. She slipped her arm beneath Jemma's armpits and began the arduous task of swimming her back to shore, battling both the strong current and erratic waves, while trying to keep both their heads above the surface. Mila kept her daughter's image in her mind, using her to keep going when her leg muscles cramped, and when she was in danger of losing hope that she could keep either of them from drowning. Just a little bit further. Each push toward shore in the dark, churning sea was painful. Was she even making progress?

Don't think about it. Just keep going.

Heart pounding, her feet finally scraped the hard bottom and she could stand. Her body was heavy, leaden with exhausted muscles and soaked clothes. Leaning over, she took a second to catch her breath, to cough out the water she had swallowed. The waves were still hitting her legs, thrusting her forward. She turned around, grasped Jemma beneath the armpits and pulled her through the whitewash until she had her stretched out on the beach, beyond the reach of the tide. At some point Jemma had shed her raincoat, so she looked so vulnerable laying there in a soaking wet T-shirt and shorts, her body completely still. Mila's muscles were shaking with fatigue as she fell beside the girl and pressed her fingers into her neck. There was a pulse, thank God, but she wasn't breathing. After everything, Mila was not going to let another girl die.

Shielding Jemma's face with her own body, Mila tilted the girl's chin back. She blew a rescue breath deep into Jemma's lungs, counted to five and then repeated the breath. It was a challenge with rain beating relentlessly on them. Mila concentrated on Jemma's face, watching for the color to return.

After the fourth breath, Jemma coughed violently, and Mila gratefully rolled her over on her side. She hovered above her, trying to give her reprieve from the wind and rain as the girl struggled to breathe. "Can you walk?" she yelled.

Jemma didn't answer. Mila didn't have time to waste, she had to find Rose. She stood, rocking in the wind and placed her hands beneath Jemma's armpits once again. This time, she had some help as Jemma pushed herself up and let Mila lead her back toward the parking lot. The struggle to just put one foot in front of the other was immense. Mila's shoes were filled with sand grinding into her soaking wet feet. They had to pause and rest every few minutes along the way, since the battle with the ocean and near-death experience had zapped both of their strength.

Finally, the brutal trek ended in the parking lot. Mila pulled open the back door of her SUV and Jemma climbed in. It wasn't until Mila was seated back behind the wheel, the door shut against the storm that she felt how badly her body was shaking. And not just because she was drenched and cold. She wouldn't let herself concentrate on that right now, though. Rose was all that mattered. She started the engine and turned to face Jemma. "Where is Rose?"

Twenty-Five

Mila handcuffed Jemma as soon as they stepped inside Gulf Shores Community Church. Jemma had sobbed during the ride there, her cries sometimes rising above the volume of the winds. But she was now completely silent, lost inside her own mind. There was no resistance. Mila led the defeated girl toward the open doors to the nave. The power was still out so it was eerily dark inside, just the flickering of candles someone had placed around the altar giving off light.

Mila had left her Glock locked in the glove box. It was resistant to water but it would need to be dried out and cleaned before she trusted using it again. So, she felt a bit exposed when she noticed Pastor Burns and Julian's outlines, dark shadows sitting in the front pew on the left and Lynnie in the front right pew. If they were all in on it together, she was outnumbered and in danger. Too late to turn back now.

She cautiously led Jemma down the aisle, watching for any movement, leaving a trail of water puddles in their wake. If the family heard them come in, they gave no indication.

Julian was the first one to turn toward them. His eyes widened and he jumped up.

"Stay where you are, Julian," Mila commanded.

He froze, his eyes locked on Jemma. He had a large purple knot on his forehead.

Pastor Burns shifted in the pew to see them but made no move to get up. His face was pale and drawn, his shoulders slumped.

"Where's Rose?" Mila asked, holding eye contact with him.

He nodded toward his wife.

Mila pushed Jemma forward so she could step in front of the pews and see Lynnie.

Relief flooded her like warm water and her legs almost gave out as she saw the little girl sleeping peacefully, cradled in a blanket in Lynnie's lap. Mila led Jemma two pews behind her father and brother, sat her down and instructed them not to talk to her.

Then she went and sat next to Lynnie. She placed the back of her hand on baby Rose's cheek, feeling the warmth, the life. She hadn't realized how much she'd feared not finding this little girl alive. How much she'd needed Rose to be alive, for a piece of Cara to live on. For Charlie to have someone to pour memories of her sister into. The relief drained the last of the energy from her battered, soaked body. Her throat began to constrict as she held back tears.

Lynnie spoke softly, without taking her eyes off of Rose. "I caught Jemma just leaving the house with the Afghan blanket tucked under her raincoat. I couldn't figure out what she was doing at first. Why she was going out in the storm... with a blanket. And eventually it hit me. She must have gotten Rose somehow. By the time we made it down here to the church, Jemma was gone." She nodded toward her family. "Julian got hit with a roof tile or something. He needs looked at by a doctor." Then she twisted so she could see Jemma, her words softer. "But she'd left Rose wrapped in the blanket behind the altar. Like a little gift."

She locked eyes with Mila, who decided to stay silent and let her talk. She needed to know exactly who knew what in this family.

"I knew you'd come as soon as you could. So, I've been soaking up every second with this precious little girl." Her eyes were glassy with tears. "I don't know what I did so wrong in life that she couldn't be mine. That I wasn't the one who carried my husband's baby." The tears broke loose and rolled down her red cheeks. "I promise you, I'd never wish harm on her mother, though. Babies need their mamas." Rose shifted in her sleep, a tiny spit bubble forming on her lips and Lynnie's attention returned to her.

Mila checked her phone. Still no service. It would probably be out until tomorrow. Now that she knew Rose was okay, she needed to get back to Charlie, get her to the hospital. But it was already a miracle she'd survived driving around in the hurricane as it was. She really should wait for the winds to die down enough to go back out safely. Especially if she took Rose in the SUV with no car seat.

Pastor Burns kept checking on Jemma, reaching back and squeezing her hand, but obeyed Mila's instructions not to talk to her. Eventually, he came over to sit beside Mila. Mila stiffened, on high alert. His voice was rough with concern. "Detective, what happened with Jemma? How did she end up with Rose? Did she take her from the sister? Is that why she's in handcuffs?"

Mila assessed him. He seemed genuinely worried, and she didn't feel threatened at the moment. She thought about her answer carefully. "Yes. She apparently wanted Rose to be a part of your family, now that everyone knew. She thought Rose would make Lynnie happy. Make her stay, I think."

Pastor Burns nodded and watched his wife stroke Rose's curls. "Do you think that's possible? That Cara's sister would let us share custody?"

Mila felt her gut tighten in protest, but she forced a smile. She still didn't know if this man had something to do with Cara's death. "You'll have to take that up with the courts." Charlie had already been granted custody, but she had no idea how a court would handle a situation like this.

Lynnie glanced up at her husband, hope in her eyes.

Mila wondered if that meant she would forgive him and stay in the marriage. But what if he did have something to do with Cara's death? Forgiving someone for being unfaithful is one thing, but she wasn't sure any marriage could survive a murder charge on top of what they'd already been through.

Mila's thoughts drifted toward her own failed marriage. The night she and Paul had drank a bottle of wine and were finally honest with each other and themselves. Love wasn't enough. They were living separate lives already, neither knowing how to build a bridge, how to open their hearts back up and be vulnerable again after all the hurt, all the distance between them. Even if they had wanted to try, there was no time in their schedules. They had agreed to cut the small thread holding them together that night and then Mila had cried until three in the morning, already regretting their decision.

A thump against the stained-glass window brought her back to the present.

She checked the time on her phone. Almost midnight. By the Weather Channel's calculations, they had about two more hours to hunker down here. Those were going to be a long two hours.

Should she try to talk to everyone while they were stuck here? Or wait until she had them back in the interview rooms where they would be recorded? Her gaze swept over the traumatized family. She should wait. She had time, so might as well do it right. First, she had to talk to Jemma. She knew for sure Jemma was there when Cara Anderson was killed. She needed to hear it from her... who else was in that lifeguard stand?

Twenty-six

When the last bands of Henry finally made their way inland, Mila had a decision to make. Should she risk taking Rose out on the flooded, debris-filled roads? Or leave her here with the Burns in the safety of the church?

After the nine plus hours of raging winds, the silence was almost eerie. Lynnie was walking Rose around showing her different things to keep her occupied. The little girl had woken up cranky and hungry. Mila watched Lynnie, deciding there was nowhere they could go with Rose, and she believed Lynnie would take good care of her. Mila would just take Jemma with her. And Julian. He needed that contusion on his head checked out.

She approached Lynnie and smiled at Rose, rubbed the little girl's soft fingers between her own. Dark lashes, wet with tears, framed her wide brown eyes. "I have to go pick up Charlie, who's injured, and get her to the hospital and Julian, too. I'll also be taking Jemma. You okay to watch Rose until I can get back?"

Lynnie's eyes lit up as she bounced Rose gently. "Of course. I'll have Collin go up to the house and see what he can find for her to eat." She glanced behind Mila, her expression growing concerned. "Are you arresting Jemma for kidnapping Rose? I know she would never put her in danger on purpose."

Well, that would be one charge. Along with theft of a firearm and firearm use in the commission of a felony. And possibly first-degree murder. "I need to take her to the station and get a statement from her. I'll let you know when you can see her."

Mila let the family hug Jemma goodbye before she loaded her back into her SUV and began the slow slog in the dark through floodwaters, palm fronds, and downed trees in the roads. She had to be extra cautious along the main road where there were possible downed power lines. There was still a light sprinkle and a gust once in a while, but nothing like the washing machine they'd been out in earlier. She felt her nervous system settling down.

"Thank God!" Charlie cried with relief when Mila walked in the door. She was still in the same position on the sofa, one lantern on the floor. "Where's Rose?"

"She's fine. She's safe. We need to get you to the hospital though." Mila gingerly helped her up and outside into the passenger seat, steadying her through a wave of dizziness and then carefully pulling the seatbelt over her bandaged side.

Charlie winced. Then she noticed Julian then Jemma in the back seat. Her face grew dark. "How could you?" she choked on her rage. "How could you put Rose in danger like that?"

Jemma stared at her through the protective plastic barrier. "I'm sorry."

Mila closed the door and slid into the driver's seat.

Julian had his head down, silent, but Jemma was still talking, seemingly finding her voice again. "I don't know why I did it. I'm sorry... Cara was my friend. I just panicked, really."

Mila was backing out of the driveway into the two feet of water rushing down the street with nowhere to go as debris covered the grates and clogged the road drains. Her headlights were the only light cutting through the dark neighborhood. She caught the look on Charlie's face. She was putting it together that Jemma had been involved in her sister's death. "Charlie, stay calm," Mila whispered, placing a hand on her knee. "Cara will get justice. Rose is safe and will go home with you. That's all that matters."

Charlie was still staring at Jemma. "You. You killed my sister. Why?" A blood-curdling scream came from Charlie: "My God...WHY!"

Mila hit the brakes on reflex. She squeezed Charlie's knee. "Hey, look at me."

Charlie's green eyes were bright with rage, with grief, her fists in tight bloodless balls. Mila knew after the rage and grief came the darkness, the depression. She hoped she had a good therapist.

Mila shook Charlie's knee, feeling the woman's body trembling beneath her palm. "She will be going to prison, I promise." Mila glanced in the back and saw that both Jemma and Julian had frozen, eyes wide with shock at the power of this small woman's fury, spewing like an erupting volcano. She turned back to Charlie. "You have to stay strong for Rose. You have to be her light."

Tears spilled down Charlie's pale cheeks, her fists slowly unclenching. She turned back, laser-focused on Jemma. "Did she suffer?"

Mila could see Jemma shaking her head vigorously in the rear-view mirror. "No. She wasn't conscious when..." Jemma stopped, not able to bring herself to say what she did out loud. Mila noticed Julian was staring at his sister, his face bloodless with shock. It didn't look like he knew, but Mila would have to get to the bottom of that during interrogation.

Charlie suddenly smacked the partition with her palm. "I will never be able to hear my sister's voice again, to hear her laugh. Rose will never feel her mother hug her again. And I will never forgive you." She turned and stared forward, the tears silently falling, mirroring the rain rolling down the windshield.

"It's okay," Jemma said. "I will never forgive myself, either."

Mila felt her own eyes stinging and had a sudden urge to hold Harper in a tight hug. Rose would be okay, though. Charlie was already equipped to protect the little girl with the fierceness of a mother.

※

After getting Charlie and Julian successfully checked into the ER, she made her way back to the station. There were already a dozen or so cars stuck in flood water even though it was almost three in the morning. She also passed a few patrol cars out checking for downed powerlines and other things that needed their attention, and a firetruck and ambulance, lights and sirens on, turning into a powerless, battered residential neighborhood.

She pulled into the partially flooded Edgewater PD parking lot. It was strange to see lights on in the building after coming from the pitch black of town. Strange, but comforting. Aiden pushed through the doors and jogged a few steps. He stopped when he saw her headlights, then splashed through the ankle-deep water, pulling her door open as she turned off the engine.

"My God... are you okay? I was just headed over to Charlie's to see if you were still there." He took in Jemma slouched in the back seat; a questioning look on his face. Then he backed up so Mila could slide out. His attention went to her limp, where she was babying the calf that had been injured by flying debris and her raw feet. "You look like hell. You hurt?"

"Just a bruise." Though if she looked as bad as she felt, she could understand his concern. "Charlie is at the ER, GSW to the abdomen, courtesy of Jemma." She opened the back door and helped Jemma slide out. Then holding the girl's forearm, she gave Aiden a meaningful look. "Got any coffee in there?"

He reached up and slid a piece of seaweed from her hair, eyes shiny with concern and questions. "Old and cold, just the way you like it."

She laughed, a much-needed release of emotion.

※

After Jemma was safely in their holding cell and a patrol unit was on the way to the church to pick up Rose, with instructions to get her checked out at the hospital, Mila sat in the conference room with Aiden, Frank and Captain Bartol. She'd changed into a dry set of clothes from her locker. She had also sucked down a bottle of water and was working on a bag of salt and vinegar chips from the vending machine, trying to give her body some fuel while she filled them in on how the evening went down. Now that she wasn't soaked to the bone, the air conditioning was a welcome reprieve. Though the more she relaxed, the more she felt every ache and sore spot in her body.

After Mila was done answering questions from the three of them, the exhaustion hit like a brick wall, and she had a hard time forming sentences.

Captain Bartol rapped her knuckles on the table, her eyes flashing with disapproval under a chunk of spiky, red bang. "Well, I assume you won't pull a stunt like that again. Going out in a damn hurricane. You could've been killed."

Mila wasn't surprised at her captain's reaction. It was a stupid thing for her to do. But she would defend it to the end of her career because Rose was safe. She lifted her shoulder half-heartedly. "But I wasn't."

Tension crackled in the air as they all stared at Captain Bartol. It had been an extremely long day, full of stress and danger, not exactly the environment in which you want to argue with a superior.

Captain Bartol's nostrils flared and then she sighed. "All right. Go on home to your little girl. Leave your weapon and I'll get you a temporary replacement. Seems like you made an effort to secure it at the house and Charlie will be fine, so the internal investigation should be short and exonerating. You can write up the report in the morning." She scanned their faces. "I expect you all back here bright and early. We have a search warrant at the Burns home to execute."

As Frank and Aiden rose, Mila cleared her throat. "Captain, I need to interview Jemma before she recovers or shuts down. I think she's ready to talk tonight. Tomorrow?" She shrugged. "Who knows."

The captain eyed her hard. But she eventually nodded. "You sure you're up for it?"

Mila really wanted to say no, to leave it for the morning and go hug her daughter. "Yes."

Aiden leaned against the wall, hands shoved in his slacks pockets. He shot Mila a boyish, tired grin. "I'll stay. Make sure you don't fall asleep mid-question."

"Thanks." She chuckled. "That's a distinct possibility."

Mila went to follow Aiden out the door when Captain Bartol stopped her and squeezed her shoulder. "Good work, Detective."

It was a rare moment of praise from the captain. Mila felt an unexpected rush of warmth. A thank you lodged behind the lump in her throat, so she just acknowledged her with a soft smile.

※

Mila sat a microwaved Styrofoam cup of coffee and a Snickers bar on the table in front of Jemma. Then she placed her notebook and pen on the table across from the teen and took a seat.

After reading Jemma her Miranda rights and having her sign them, Mila glanced at the camera to make sure the red light was on and began.

"All right, Jemma. The sooner we get to the truth, the sooner you can rest. It's been a harrowing day and you must be exhausted. I know I am."

Jemma's gaze was unfocused somewhere behind Mila. Her expression was spacey and slack. She was lost in her own thoughts.

Mila touched her hand. "Why don't you take a sip of coffee. It'll warm you up." She watched, hoping the act of fueling her body would ground Jemma, bring her back to the present.

Jemma slowly lifted the cup to her mouth and took a sip. Then another. She blinked and sat the cup down, but kept her hands wrapped around it.

Mila rested her elbows on the table, leaning into Jemma's space. "I'm going to be honest with you here, Jemma. I know you were there the night Cara died. So, start from the beginning. Take me through what happened that day."

"Okay." Jemma lifted her gaze to meet Mila's. There was plenty of raw pain there, but no fight left. "Dad was supposed to meet Cara at the beach that night. At the lifeguard stand." A shiver moved through her body. "I overheard him at the house, on the phone. From their conversation I knew Cara wanted him to come clean to Mom. Tell her about Rose. Which would destroy her. Destroy our family."

Mila held up her hand to interrupt. It sounded like Jemma had already known about Rose. "When did you find out your dad had fathered Rose?"

Jemma sat up straighter, her eyes finally showing some expression. She seemed eager to tell this part of the story, unburden herself. *How long had this secret been eating away at her?*

"Cara had sent Dad an email way back when she found out she was pregnant. She emailed his work account, which I help him answer emails, so I saw it. He deleted it, but it was too late. I didn't tell him I saw it. I didn't really know what to do." She started picking at a raw cuticle, her words tumbling out faster. "I ended up finding Cara in Tampa. It wasn't hard. She'd mentioned she worked at the Spookeasy Lounge in the email. I just had to get my driver's license. It's why I would take the car without Dad knowing. I just wanted to see what kind of person she was. If she was lying. I wanted to talk to her, but I kept chickening out."

So, it was Jemma who'd been following Cara. "Okay, so when you overheard the phone call your dad had with Cara the night she died, what did you decide to do about it?"

"Well." Jemma chewed at the skin on her thumb, thinking. Finally, she dropped her hands to the table. "I knew I had to talk to Cara. Convince her not to ruin our family. I thought she would listen to me because we were friends. But I didn't realize... I didn't know she thought Dad raped her. I guess I'd be pissed, too." She suddenly looked sheepish. "Anyway, I found the picnic basket in the back of the car with the wine. I guess Dad was planning on sweet-talking her, being nice to try and get her to not ruin our family. But, I could tell by the way he acted all depressed when he got off the phone with her, that he knew it was a long shot."

"Then?" Mila prompted when she looked like Jemma was getting lost in her thoughts again.

Cara's gaze slid to the floor. "Then I got an idea."

"What was your idea?"

Jemma glanced up through her lashes, guilt flashing in her eyes. "I gave Dad a teaspoon of Ipecac syrup, so he'd get sick and have to stay home." She pushed her hands into her hair, rested her elbows on the table and dropped her head. "I know, I know. It was a horrible thing to do. He got really sick."

Mila jotted that down. So, Pastor Burns really was sick that night. Which meant that Lynnie was telling the truth, too, and was home taking care of him. That left Julian as a possible accomplice. She folded her arms and sat back in the chair, letting the silence stretch out, letting Jemma stew in the guilt of making her dad sick. When Jemma started to squirm in the chair and make whimpering noises under her breath, Mila nudged her to keep going. "So you made sure your dad had to stay home. What happened after that?"

Jemma hugged herself and rubbed her bare arms roughly. Self-soothing behavior. She was getting really uncomfortable. Mila had to make sure she didn't shut down before getting the whole story. "You're doing great, Jemma. Your dad would be proud of you for being so brave right now. What did you do next?"

Jemma's hands were trembling as she clutched the Styrofoam cup full of now-cold coffee. She took in a deep breath, blew it out and continued. "I swiped Grandpa's Xanax from the bathroom. Figured if I got there and Cara wouldn't listen to reason, I could put it in the wine and knock her out. Then I could go to the house and take Rose." She glanced up. "I mean, I wasn't going to hurt Rose. But if she thought Rose was in danger here in Edgewater, she'd never feel safe. She'd have to leave, right?"

Jemma's inexperience with people showed here. No way Cara would've just quietly left town. But again, desperate people do stupid things. Mila kept her tone soft, understanding. "Sounds like you didn't want to hurt Cara or Rose. So, what went wrong?"

Jemma suddenly pushed herself out of the chair and began pacing the small room, arms crossed tight against her chest. Mila stayed on guard as she followed her movements.

"Cara was so mad when she saw me. I've never seen her that mad. She thought Dad sent me instead of coming himself and kept calling him a coward and other really bad names."

Her voice was rising, her face flushed as she relived the moments that would change her life forever. "I had put the Xanax in the wine bottle as soon as we opened it. And Cara was so mad, she was drinking it straight from the bottle. I started to worry I'd put too much Xanax in it." She leaned her back against the wall, arms still crossed. "The more she drank, the more truth came out. She wanted to ruin Dad's life. She wanted Mom to know he raped her. She wanted him fired from the church. She was going to go to the police about the rape." She flung her arms out in front of her, her eyes welling up with tears. "She was talking about Dad like he was a demon that needed to be destroyed. I mean, he made a mistake... we're all human. God forgives us. So, why couldn't she forgive him?"

Mila knew that he had never apologized to Cara for that night because he had a different version of events in his head. He probably asked God's forgiveness but not Cara's. She wondered briefly if Cara's death could've been averted by that one simple thing. An apology. They would never know.

Jemma began her pacing again. She was now on the verge of hysterics, the tears flowing, her nose running. "She wouldn't agree to let it go, let us live in peace. So when she finally passed out, I knew what I had to do." A sob broke through her words. "I had to." Deep, belly-shaking sobs erupted from the teen as she collapsed onto the floor.

Mila rose and gently helped her up, leading her to sit back in the chair. Jemma didn't even seem to notice she'd moved. Her grief was all-consuming, and she was drowning in it. Mila had to pull her out. "Jemma, let's get through this. Then you'll never have to talk about it again. It will be over." Not true, but a necessary lie. Jemma's cheeks were bright patches of red, and snot ran from her nose. Mila plucked some Kleenex from the box and pressed the tissue into Jemma's hands. She squeezed the teen's hands between her own. They were ice cold. "Come on, Jemma. Let's get this done."

Jemma nodded slowly, her gaze locked on the table. "I thought about pulling Cara into the ocean, to make it look like she drowned accidentally, but she was too heavy." Her words were robotic now, void of inflection. "I couldn't get her down the stairs. Then I saw... I saw the knife on her keychain. There was this girl that I knew in foster care, killed herself that way. Cut her arms with a knife in the tub. So I knew I could make it look like a suicide." Her mouth moved like she was talking but no words came. *Was she praying?* Mila squeezed Jemma's hands again. She finally pushed the words out. "I didn't know... didn't know there would be so much... blood." Her voice hitched on the last word. Panic flashed in her eyes, which were almost swollen shut now. "I promise, she didn't wake up, didn't feel a thing. I didn't want to hurt her." Her breathing grew erratic, and her voice cracked. "I don't really remember how I got back to the car. I just know I needed to see Rose afterwards. To tell her I was sorry that her mom wasn't coming home. I had grown to think of her as my sister. But she wasn't in her crib. Just like when I came to get her tonight."

So it was Jemma who removed the hurricane shutter on Rose's window. "Julian...he wasn't with you? He didn't help you in any way?"

She shook her head. "Only me, Cara and God were there." Her gaze shifted to meet Mila's for the first time. Her pupils dilated with fear. "Do you think God can forgive me?"

"That's between you and Him." Something in the way Jemma's face crumpled with despair reminded Mila of her daughter. She reached over and rested a hand on Jemma's forearm. "Your father told me that God can forgive anything, as long as you're alive to ask for forgiveness."

When Jemma was tucked back into the holding cell, Aiden walked Mila to her SUV. They'd both taken off their shoes and rolled up their pant legs to navigate the flood waters. The storm had swept away the humidity and left crisp air in its wake. The sound of the powerful generator running behind the station was the only thing interrupting the silence.

"Two young women's lives destroyed." Aiden sighed as a breeze ruffled his curls. "So tragic. Sometimes I hate this job."

Mila glanced up where a glowing white half-moon was finally visible in the clearing sky. *Where was the light in this situation?* Rose. She unlocked the door and threw her messenger bag and shoes in the passenger seat, then turned to Aiden. "Yes, but Rose survived, and we were part of that. Part of getting justice for Cara. You can feel good about that."

He dug his own keys out of his pocket. "I'm too tired to feel good about anything right now. But.. tomorrow is a new day. See ya in a few hours, Harlow."

Twenty-seven

Mila should have just made the short drive back home for the night, but she really needed to see Harper, to know she was okay. So instead she carefully navigated the thirty-minute drive inland to Paul's house, hydroplaning and stopping to remove tree branches blocking her way more than once.

When she finally turned onto Paul's street, she saw Kittie's dark blue Subaru in the driveway and her chest loosened, her shoulders relaxed. She also chastised herself silently as she noted her own disappointment that Paul still wasn't home.

Kittie opened the screen door when she saw the headlights. She was wearing a thin, sleeveless nightgown and held a camping lantern to help Mila navigate her way to the front door. "You look like you had a rough night. Hungry?" she asked quietly.

Mila shook her head. She was sweaty, sore and exhausted but not hungry. "Just need to see Harper."

They moved into the living room. It was littered with half-finished craft projects and snack food. A battery-powered fan was blowing toward the sofa. The two women kept their arms around each other as they stared down at Harper sleeping there, her mouth open in a tiny snore, her arm flung over Oscar, who only wagged the tip of his tail in greeting. He seemed to not want to disturb his ward's sleep, either.

"She didn't want to sleep in her room. Wanted to wait for you out here."

Harper shifted and opened her eyes. They met Mila's and a dimple appeared in her cheek. "Hi, Mom. You made it."

Mila leaned down and pressed a kiss to her forehead, getting a lick from Oscar as she did. "Yes, I'm here. Go back to sleep."

"Love you," Harper sighed, closing her eyes.

"I'll get you a pillow and sheet," Kittie whispered. "You can catch a few hours of sleep yourself."

Mila walked quietly to the hall bathroom. There was a battery-powered lantern already turned on, sitting on the sink. She used the toilet then went to wash her hands. The toothbrush holder caught her eye. One blue toothbrush... and one pink one. It wasn't Harper's. She had an electric one. So did Kittie. She glanced at herself in the mirror and saw the devastation in her own eyes. No. No, one toothbrush wasn't proof. Heart beating, and before she could stop herself, she kneeled down and opened the cabinet door below the sink. A box of Tampax sat in front of Paul's shaving kit. Her stomach dropped.

He was seeing someone. Why didn't he tell her?

She leaned against the counter. It had been five years, what did she expect. Why should he tell her? It wasn't really her business, right? Well, it was if he introduced this woman to Harper. She'd have to talk to him about that.

Nauseous and achy, she set her phone alarm for seven a.m., hoping the battery would last that long. She forgot to charge it at the station. Then she laid the sheet down, so she didn't stick to the brown leather and curled up on Paul's loveseat.

All she wanted was to close her eyes and leave behind thoughts of murdered women, the sound of Henry tearing through Edgewater, and the image of Paul in some other woman's arms. But unfortunately, they all followed her into her dreams.

※　　※　　※

Printed in Great Britain
by Amazon

46288125R10133